KEVIN DEER

& The 12 Mistresses Of The Zodiac

KEVIN DEER

& THE 12 MISTRESSES OF THE ZODIAC

SECRETS AT THE OBSERVATORY

ISAAC J. REED

REDWOOD PUBLISHING, LLC

First paperback edition, February 2019

Printed in the United States of America

This is a work of fiction. Names, characters, places, and incidents either are the product of the author's imagination or are used fictitiously. Any resemblance to actual persons, living or dead, events, or locales is entirely coincidental.

Book design by Redwood Publishing, LLC
www.redwooddigitalpublishing.com

ISBN 978-1-947341-41-8 (paperback)
ISBN 978-1-947341-42-5 (ebook)

Library of Congress Control Number: 2019930580

Dedicated to LOVE

I dedicate this book to so many people – you've all made an impact on my writing journey and for that, I thank you.

My Grandmother, Maggie Bailey
My Mother, Cheryl Bailey
My Niece, April Graison
My Mentor, Christopher Callaghan
My Big Sister, Cathy Bonn
My Bromigo, Simon Harrison
My Mentor, Robert Aranda
My Big Brother, Ismail Mayegun
My Bromigo, Parul Gujral
My Schatz, Sara A.-A Forutan
My Uncle, Marshal Bailey
My Godmother, Claudia Taurean
My High School Advisor, Etsuko Kubo
My Mentor, Lisa Hoover
My Mentee, Delvon Morgan
My Painter, Adrijana Cernic
My Bromigo, Abe Wharton
My Godmother, Dorothy Webb
My Family, 28th Street
My Nephew, Jacob Aranda
My Nephew, Hunter Diaz
My Website Guru, Vikrant Kirar
My Brother, Cobi Obiese
My Bromigo, Myles Chatman
My Spanish Teacher, Amber Moyle
My Hero and Math Teacher, Allen Saigen
My Physics Teacher, Amanda Kruger Hill
My Running Buddy, Sara Stratton & Redwood Publishing

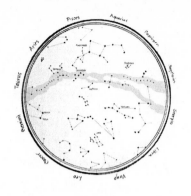

CHAPTER I
—IN THE BEGINNING—

Most love stories end in one of two ways. Both versions start with an optimistic and pure lover who pursues love with a general disregard for logic and reason. However, one version ends with the optimist finding love so pure that he or she is glowing, brighter than any star in the sky, and filled with happiness, whereas in the second version, the optimistic soul is not so lucky, and he or she is met with painful heartbreak. In this version, the optimistic lover tries again and again until love *is* found.

In the end, love will be found sooner or later.

But what if there were a third outcome for the optimistic lover? What if there were a love so strong that it attracted every enemy to dilute its harmony? What if a love story never actually ended in love at all?

For Kevin Deer, a simple small-town boy and hopeless romantic, this third outcome was unimaginable. Unlike most adolescents and his peers, his heart could not be dimmed. He had inherited a sense of wholesomeness from a decade of hallmark movies and romantic sitcoms that he and his parents used to watch together before they passed. Perhaps that was his engine. He held tightly on to the image of love those movies created—it was his way of keeping his parents close.

Kevin recognized the hard work and dedication that both parties had to commit to in order to keep their love growing and strong. But he also believed there was something else that drove true love, and that was fate. Kevin believed there were forces in the universe that had such a magnetic pull that no matter what, love would find its way to the forefront. But he knew that fate didn't equal perfect. Fate just secured the time and the place. As gallant as his ambition was, it could very well be his undoing as he embarked on a love journey of his own. On a night when true love was meant to be an accomplishment, it represented dire misfortune.

☙

There was a violent sense of horror that night. Besides the blood running down Kevin's shirt, there was an incredible hurt running through his body. Lying there in the mud, he looked up at his antagonist. The rain made it hard to see her clearly. He could see just her eyes, filled with secrets, lies, and hate. But how could one such as Kevin have come to such a gruesome end? All he'd ever wanted was true love. Instead, he was met with all the fear that love works to fight against.

"Please don't do this," Kevin said, as he groaned in pain, soaked in his own blood.

It was all he could manage. The fall from the stairs felt like it had crushed one of his lungs, and he could hardly speak. In just one year he had turned what was meant to be a journey of self-discovery and to find true love into an erratic and dangerous adventure—one that now put his and his friends' lives at stake.

Could this be the end? Kevin thought. He looked to his side and grimaced. He saw Claire—she was helpless, much more helpless than he had ever seen her. And Sam, well, he was either already dead or unconscious now.

Kevin couldn't believe what he had done—he was guilty of putting his best friends in this predicament. Shame and anger began to well up inside him. It brought about a sense of ownership as he anticipated what would happen next. It was at that moment that he knew what he must do.

He turned back to look at his murderer. "Look. I'm truly ... truly and deeply sorry for all of the hurt that I caused you," Kevin said.

"Shut up!" his attacker screamed. "Don't you think you've already done enough, Kevin? I love you. Do you even under-stand that? I love you!" She craved a reciprocal response.

After hearing those words, Kevin, still struggling to stay conscious, felt a strange sense of achievement—along with deep regret—at hearing those words. He had done it. He had accomplished what he had set out to do from the start. But his sense of nobility wouldn't allow him this victory. Even his friends knew that. He chose to continue his sacrifice.

"Do you have nothing to say? I've poured my heart out to you," she said; her voice was shaking. "Now tell me what you're thinking," she demanded, her eyes desperately searching Kevin's, waiting for his response.

"I … I can't. I'm sorry," Kevin said. "I … don't love you."

Her eyes were wide with horror as she tried to measure each word coming out of his mouth. She was desperate for it—his admission. But this wasn't it. Her mouth hung open, and for a moment, it seemed as if she were convincing herself that those words hadn't just come out of Kevin's mouth.

But Kevin kept going. "I don't feel the same way," Kevin said looking to his friends. "I just don't. I can't lie to you. I can't lie to myself. I've done enough of that. Please. Let them go. Do what you need to with me. Just, please leave them out of it. Please."

Her eyes darted back and forth between Kevin and his two helpless friends. It was clear she had lost all control and all hope.

"You … you asshole! I loved you!" she screamed.

That next moment slowed down, and a sweet melody began to play in Kevin's head. Every element played its part to carry the tune. The rain, the moon, they all played their part as she raised her weapon. Kevin lowered his eyes.

"I hope she was worth it, Kevin," she said. The metallic black of her gun glittered in the moonlight.

The next set of events happened so quickly that Kevin couldn't piece them all together, but they exposed a deep sorrow. From the corner of Kevin's eyes, a shadow appeared and leaped straight toward him. Then, the popping sound of an old handgun going off like a large firework on the Fourth of July. This was followed by heavy breaths and deep panting.

Kevin looked up and saw panic in his murderer's eyes. He looked back down at Claire. Her tears matched the rain. He pulled her close, but it was all too little too late.

☽

About one year earlier...

There was a time when life was not gripped with the looming presence of death. In fact, one year ago had been a time of celebration for the then high school junior at Cambridge High School Boarding Academy. It was a joyful time, and one that made it easier to appreciate the banners and confetti that glistened in the sunlight. It was the start of Winter Break—between Fall/Winter Semester and Spring/Summer Semester—and the academy was throwing its annual "Senior Recruitment Day," an all-day event for the junior class. With only one semester left in their junior year, Senior Recruitment Day was meant to excite the junior class about their upcoming senior year, provide guidance on college applications, and help them to determine a path for their future. Representatives from the most prestigious of universities were sitting at booths, ready to answer questions about their respective college campuses; career counselors were reviewing resumes and making suggestions as to the best classes to take in senior year; and well-known Fortune 500 companies and start-up companies were accepting internship applications.

"So, you ready for your speech?"

Kevin looked up from his flashcards to see Claire Wong standing in front of him with a grin on her face. Her smile was bright—the years of Crest Whitestrips had given her teeth the same shine seen on cartoon princesses. Her face still had childhood innocence, which made the tomboy all the more charming and easily trusted by all. Her dimples only appeared when she smiled wide or when she laughed. She picked a prep school jacket that was one size too large for her, and her year-old, dirty and tattered sneakers stood out over her otherwise clean uniform.

"Yeah, not even close." Kevin laughed nervously. "Ugh, where's Sam? He's supposed to be here by now." Kevin's eyes scrunched together to form worry wrinkles on his forehead. He was an all American boy—his light brown hair looked like sun-bleached wood, combed back in his usual prep boy style, and his baby blue eyes sparkled like the ocean on a summer day. He wore his usual white Oxford button-down shirt, which always looked as though it had been freshly steam-pleated minutes before.

"Sam?" Claire said. "Why? He probably stopped for snacks, knowing him." She rolled her eyes, which were a deep chestnut color. "Hey, you okay? You seem a bit ... well, nervous."

Kevin ignored her question and looked back down to his flashcards.

"I'm worried about you, Kevin," Claire said, placing her hand on his arm. "I know coming to this school was a big transition for you, especially after your parents died, and then after Susan ..." she trailed off as Kevin closed his eyes at the mention of Susan's name. "Kevin, I'm saying this as one of your best friends standing for the last ten years, Susan's a complete idiot for wanting to call things off with you. I'm sure she'll regret it." Claire gave Kevin's arm a squeeze, as if to reassure him.

"Thanks. I appreciate it," Kevin said.

"Besides, there's a whole lot of fish in the sea at Cambridge," Claire teased.

They smiled at each other. Kevin's smile sparkled in the sun—it was mesmerizing.

"Hey look … Claire … I, umm …" Kevin looked at Claire, wanting to be honest with her. "There's something I should tell you about the whole Susan thing."

"Hey, sorry I'm late guys," Sam shouted, breathing heavily as he ran up and pushed between the two friends. "You wouldn't believe the amount of construction in the bike lanes these days. Absolute nightmare."

Sam pushed his thick-rimmed black glasses up his nose. He was heavier than Kevin, and fit awkwardly into his uniform clothes. He pulled at his cable-knit uniform sweater vest, trying to stretch it down, and fumbled with his uniform tie, which he could never seem to get right. His wavy hair had been trimmed close to his head. He was drenched in sweat. Regardless, he was proud that he had managed to accomplish Kevin's errand and make it back to the ceremony with time to spare.

"Geez Sam," Kevin said as he put his hand out and waved his fingers open and closed, signaling he was ready to receive something he was owed. "I needed this about an hour ago."

"Hi Sam," Claire interjected. She was annoyed he hadn't acknowledged her standing there.

"Hey Claire," Sam replied, looking quickly at her and then back at Kevin as he put a small black velvet box in Kevin's hand. "I know I said I'd be here sooner, but the shop was impossible to find. I hope I picked up the right one you ordered."

"Jewelry store?" Claire asked, her eyes widening.

"Uhh ... the ring, obviously," Sam replied, annoyed at Claire's question. Looking at Claire's face and seeing her forehead wrinkled with confusion, he realized his mistake. "Wait ... you didn't know about it?"

Claire stared at them both with her mouth open. Kevin shuffled his notecards in his hands and dug the toe of his left white Converse sneaker into the grass. His fair skin had turned bright red—he could feel the warmth of embarrassment on his cheeks. He could feel Claire's eyes on him, and he knew she was waiting for an answer.

"I tried to tell you just now," Kevin said, looking back at her.

"Kevin Deer," Claire demanded. "Are you proposing to Susan? Are you serious?" Claire poked her pointer finger in his chest. "Kevin, the girl completely blew you off. All because her rich and pretentious parents didn't like you. And you're like sixteen years young last time I checked."

"Claire, relax, it's not an engagement ring. It's a promise ring. It's totally different."

"Kevin," Claire said tonelessly. "She ... broke *up* with you."

"I know, and I get it," Kevin said. "But maybe this will fix things and show Susan *and* her parents how serious I am."

Both Claire and Sam looked down, and there was a moment of tense silence.

"Look, guys," Kevin said. "I know the break-up was really tough on me. And you guys had to pick up the pieces. But I'm sure Susan is the one. I felt something special with her. I love her. Isn't that what life is all about? To find that person that makes you want to be better ... the person that gives you a reason for taking leaps of faith?"

"This is probably more of a jump from a hundred-story building than it is a leap," Claire said.

"Hey, we have your back man," Sam said, and put his arm around Kevin. He gave Claire a dirty look. Sam didn't get mad often, so Claire knew he meant it when she got that look.

"Right," Claire muttered. "We have your back on this ... I guess."

"Thanks," Kevin said.

"So, did you figure out how you were going to do it?" Sam asked. "I vote you do it in front of everyone once she walks off the stage. Now that's magic."

"I thought about that," Kevin said. "But it's not good enough."

"Oh boy," Claire sighed.

"See ... when Susan broke up with me, she said that her parents felt I wasn't 'Cambridge material,'" Kevin said. "I feel like I need to prove to them that I have the confidence of a Cambridge man, you know. So, after my speech, they'll change their minds about me. I know it."

"Kevin, I'm pretty sure that's not..." Claire started to say.

Sam interrupted by clearing his throat and looked at Claire before she could finish. His angry eyes met hers, and he subtly shook his head back and forth, a signal to stop what she was saying.

"Er ... okay. Sure. I'm sure that's exactly what they'll want," Claire said, rolling her eyes at Sam and giving him a scowl.

"I'm going to do this big," Kevin said, pushing his shoulders back and taking a deep breath as he shoved the black velvet ring box into the pocket of his light beige Chino pants. His blue eyes were full of renewed energy.

He squeezed his hands into fists, looked at Claire and Sam, and said with a confident nod, "I'm going to do it right after my speech."

☽

Eventually the junior students were joined by their parents, who had been invited by the academy so that the students could receive family support as they made choices for their future. It was time for the dean to give his speech, thanking the families for their attendance. The students and their families gathered and sat in the rows of cheap white chairs—uniforms of navy blue and khaki blanketed the field. It was a moment of promise. For three friends in particular, it was a day that would dictate their future, in more ways than one.

Kevin was already sitting on the stage. As the junior class Charter Scholarship winner, he had been awarded a free ride at the Academy for his junior and senior year, and he was responsible for giving the students a speech after the dean.

"Geez. What's your issue Claire?" Sam grunted, elbowing her in the ribs as they walked to find their seats. They had told their parents not to come—each came from families that were a little rough around the edges, and so both were used to making adult decisions for themselves without the support of adults. "You know how much he likes Susan. This could be his one shot to get her back."

Claire wouldn't dare tell Sam the reason for her conflict. He would never understand. In fact, Claire did not fully understand the conflict herself. She had known Kevin for over ten years, long before they attended Cambridge together, and they had always been the picture of a solid, celebrated friendship. On nights when her parents fought, she would often visit Kevin's house and climb through his window for safety. She fondly remembered when he would cook her pasta after she came over—using a terrible Italian accent, he would pretend to be a hotel concierge and serve her as if she were a noble who had traveled from afar. She would be stressed from her parents arguing, and he wouldn't even question it—he would just make her food and ask if he could "fluff her pillows, bella bella." They were more than just neighbors or friends. They were partners in life—the kind of best friends some people never have.

And yet, as the vines of maturity often grow and reveal new buds, Claire began to have deeper feelings for Kevin—feelings of shy admiration. And though she was considered the pragmatic one of the group, her heart's deepest secret proved otherwise.

"Ugh. Don't you think I know that, Sam?" Claire folded her arms. "I mean, it's only obvious he's crazy about her."

"So then what's your deal?" Sam asked.

"I just … I just don't want to see him get hurt again."

"He's not … he won't …" Sam put his arm around Claire's shoulder, in an attempt to reassure her (and maybe even himself) that their third musketeer would be okay.

"Sam," Claire said, "you weren't there, okay? You didn't see the look on his face after she called it off. It was like … like he'd just lost everything in the world. Kevin. The nicest guy ever. How could she be so cold like that? He's crazy for going after her again."

Sam paused. "Claire, you remember that day when we all went camping for Kevin's birthday? It was in the worst mosquito-ridden place possible. Remember? We had bites for days."

"How could I forget? I was so mad at both of you on that trip. I couldn't believe you ate all of my snacks," Claire said, giving Sam a light shove.

Sam laughed and blushed, adjusting his glasses.

"So what's your point, snack thief?" Claire said.

"My point is … that night we sat by the fire … Kevin was feeling lonely. It was his first birthday after his parents died. And we made a pact, Claire. To always support and be there for each other. No matter what. Remember?"

"I remember," Claire said. She brushed her straight jet-black hair out of her face and twirled a piece of it around her index finger.

"Okay," Sam said. "So that's my point. I get that the situation with Susan is a bit crazy. Hell … it's *a lot* crazy. But Kevin doesn't need an 'I told you so.' He needs his friends."

"God, fine. I just hope you're right about this one, Dr. Phil," Claire said.

Sam felt pride in getting his point across. His short and lumpy frame stood tall for the first time. However, inside he was torn. Sam had never been what most people would deem a 'lady's man.' In fact, he was far from it. But there was one lady in particular whose attention he was hoping to catch. It was Claire. Not a day went by when he didn't think about how she had been the one to save him from receiving a grueling atomic wedgie on his first day at Cambridge. It was on the same day that the three of them became friends. He held her friendship more dearly than any other. Perhaps Sam had selfish motives for supporting Kevin in this crazy move—if Kevin was in love with Susan, maybe that would inspire Claire to look for love as well. And then Sam would be there.

He stared at Claire—she didn't even know how beautiful she was, which only made her more loveable. He snapped out of his daydream so as not to get his hopes up.

"Want to grab these?" Claire said pointing at a couple of empty chairs.

"Sure," Sam said. He looked at her once again before the festivities started.

Just as Claire had a secret, so did he. Three friends, two secrets, and one future made for an intriguing situation. Only time would tell of its revelation.

※

"Attention, ladies and gentlemen," said the dean, tapping on the microphone in front of him. His microphone was working loud and clear. "Please take your seats. Senior Recruitment Day is about to commence."

This was no ordinary ceremony. For Cambridge High Boarding Academy's staff, and its junior class students especially, this ceremony centered around the junior students having just one more year at the academy. After graduating, they would go on to get their degrees, hopefully from prestigious universities. This year, as the crowd gathered around to witness, Kevin grew nervous. He wiped his sweaty hands on his pants and tried to go over his speech notes one more time as the ceremonial tunes played in the background. Perhaps it was a combination of the sun beating down on him and his unsettled stomach, but he couldn't make out the faces in the crowd. He squinted to look harder, but he could only see their smiles. He took a deep breath. It was enough to erase the uneasy swirl in his stomach for just a brief moment.

He reached for the ring in his pants pocket. The swirls came back and his mind raced. Kevin had never taken such a huge risk, but he knew he had to do it. Every inch of his body burned with incandescent zeal as he finally saw the very reason for those swirls. There she was—Susan Rey. She was even more stunning when the beams of sun reflected off of her red hair, giving it a burnt orange glow, like the sunsets they used to watch together. Kevin knew she was "The One." He could feel it. He smiled at her, hoping she couldn't see his nervousness through his gritted teeth. But she returned his smile from across the stage and everything felt right again. Susan, his friends waving at him from the audience, and the new shiny platinum in his pants pocket. Kevin silently convinced himself that Susan being there that day meant the universe was rooting for him to make his next move. This was his time.

"And now we are going to hear from our Charter Scholarship winner—Kevin Deer." The dean cleared his throat and Kevin snapped back to reality. He walked up and shook the dean's hand with pride. "Knock them dead, my boy," Dean Keller said as he squeezed Kevin's hand.

Kevin rubbed his stomach one last time and tapped his notecards on the podium. Taking a second glance, he realized the picture on the jumbotron was much larger than he had thought. All he could do was hope that it didn't make his ears look too big. He took another deep breath. This one allowed him to focus on the people who mattered.

"Thanks everyone. Uhh … As Dean Keller said, my name is Kevin Deer and I'm the winner of this year's Charter Scholarship. I'm really grateful. Well, maybe perhaps not so grateful to be sweating bullets right now …" Kevin paused to allow the crowd some time to laugh. "No seriously. All jokes aside. This is a moment we've all been waiting for. A moment we can all share. In just a little over one year from now, we'll all be graduating Cambridge." Kevin glanced at Susan, and then at his friends. "There's a quote that I recently came across. It's by someone we all probably know—the Dalai Lama. He said, 'Great love and great achievements involve great risk.' My fellow students, we all are here to achieve. And we all took risks to do it. Many of us left our families and old friends behind as we transferred to a new town to live on campus at Cambridge Academy. We had to adjust to earlier class times, year-round schooling, and living with new people. A lot of risk. Every time one of us volunteered to solve the problem of the day in Mrs. Grandule's mathematics class. Every time we chose to try the new sandwich featured on the campus bistro …" Kevin gave the audience another opportunity to laugh. "Every time we turned down the opportunity to go home for the weekend and instead stayed here to study. We all took risks. And they all meant something special. And they've all paid off. I am sure you know the feeling, like after opening your report card after a big week of studying. It feels great.

"But ... the most special risk of them all is the one I discovered just this past year. I'd like to invite Susan Rey to join me for this actually."

Kevin's heart was pounding at this point, and he could feel the thumping in his ears. He felt as though anyone standing close enough to him would have seen the vulnerable lump of flesh vibrating in his chest. But as uncomfortable as he was about his effort, there was someone he hoped would notice it. He reached for Susan's hand as she walked up with a nervous grin.

"Susan Rey ... You've been ... Wow, I'm actually doing this," Kevin said as he cleared his throat. "You have been one of the greatest parts of my life."

"Kevin what are you do—" Susan muttered.

Kevin didn't allow her to finish. "In fact, it kind of goes back to what the Dalai Lama says: *love* is something that involves great risk," he said. "So, I guess I'm taking his advice in this case." His gaze was fixed on Susan's eyes. Her eyes were the color of caramel, flecked with dark brown spots that glistened in the right light. But if he had looked closer, he would have seen the cloud of confusion that now came over her face.

Kevin pulled out the ring box, and Susan's eyes bulged out of her head. She ripped her hand out of his and placed it on her forehead. He looked at her deeper, in the midst of all the gasps and *awws* that followed him dropping to his knee. This moment for him couldn't have been more perfect. He was ready to risk it all. He wanted to do it for her.

"Susan Rey ... I know what you're thinking—we're still too young to get married. I agree. So this isn't an engagement ring—it's a promise ring, a symbol of my commitment to you. Will you make me the happiest guy in the world? Will you promise to one day marry me?"

Susan looked at her parents, who were in the crowd paying keen attention. "Kevin, I … I … I can't. I'm sorry." She backed away waving her hands in front of her as if she were in front of a car that wasn't stopping.

And there it was—that feeling you get when you've had too many feature sandwiches from the campus bistro. Kevin felt miserable. His stomach dropped. He felt his heart shatter into a thousand pieces. To make matters worse, her rejection prompted a startled reaction from the crowd. A few jocks began shouting "NEEEEXT" and "REJECTED" loudly in unison. Their parents tried to quiet them down. Those who were more polite just sat in silence, whispering behind their hands to one another. As Susan ran off the stage, the jumbotron seemed to magnify everything. Kevin looked into the crowd. All he could see was the faces of Claire and Sam. Their look said it all. His risk had turned into a disaster.

֍

The sun was finally setting on the long and drawn out afternoon of celebration. Sam and Claire walked toward Kevin, who was sitting alone in one of the cheap foldout chairs. His notecards were on the ground in front of him, and his shoulders were slumped forward, with his arms hanging between his open legs—it looked as if the world had ended. They had never seen their friend so low. All they wanted to do was make things better. But before they could offer up support and encouraging words, Susan appeared and walked up to Kevin first. Sam and Claire stopped walking.

"Hey," Susan said.

"Hi," Kevin said, still staring at his shoes.

"You okay?" Susan asked.

"Seriously?" Kevin grunted. "How could I be okay? I looked like a complete idiot up there."

Susan paused and placed her hand on Kevin's shoulder. "Look, Kevin. I didn't mean to hurt you. It's just that ... I thought we were clear on things. That we were broken up."

"I guess I thought I could convince you to take me back," Kevin said.

The purple and orange in the sky had grown deeper. The wind had stopped. Despite all the joy that had been shared between loved ones that day, somberness now took the lead. It was haunting, yet elegant. As Susan and Kevin glanced at his note cards lying on the grass, they both knew the truth in all of the serenity.

"Kevin," Susan said. "I want the best for you. I do. But this," she pointed at his notecards and then at the stage, "This isn't love. You can't just make some grand gesture like that and expect me to go against my parents' wishes. It just doesn't work that way. I guess what I'm saying is ... goodbye, Kevin."

She turned and trotted away without so much as a look back. That was it. The risk, the reward, the glory: it was all just mythical nonsense. Kevin now saw why love was indeed a risk.

Susan's departure was the sign Claire and Sam needed to continue their walk to Kevin. "You okay, Kevin?" Claire asked when they reached him.

Sam went to pat Kevin's back to comfort him. He saw the tears welling up in Kevin's eyes and did his best to keep from breaking down himself.

"It's not over," Kevin muttered. "I can't give up on love. I won't. Not after today."

"We won't let you, buddy," Sam said as he and Claire sat down in the chairs next to their friend. We will help you find 'the one.'" Nobody said anything after Sam's declaration. The campus field was pretty much empty now. Just the three of them remained, yet their hearts had never felt more full. The camaraderie these friends shared could beat anything. It was as clear as the stars that were starting to peek through the sky.

"Kevin I ... I'm so sorry," Claire said, doing her best to be strong for her friend. "This isn't permanent you know. You've got a lot of good things going on. You'll be a senior soon enough. Then it's on to college—we've talked about it for years, and now it's practically right around the corner. And for the record ... you are the bravest guy I know."

"Yeah?" Kevin asked.

"Hell yeah," Claire said and flashed Kevin a smile. "It took a lot of guts to do what you did. You kicked butt up there. Hey ... just promise me one thing will you?"

"What's that?" Kevin asked, his countenance was still low.

"Promise me you'll make Sam help fight all the girls off you this year..." Claire said, lightly punching Kevin in the arm.

"Hey!" Sam said. "I can take them on by myself you know. I'm pretty tough when I want to be. *And* charming."

They all laughed. It was the first time that day they had let go of all their anxiety. Despite the sad outcome, they knew they all needed this. It was like a reset on their friendship. What they didn't know was that their greatest adventure was just around the corner.

☽

"Welcome guys to our last semester as juniors! Before we know it, senior year will start, and we will all be on our way to college!" Sam said as he opened his arms wide to showcase the Cambridge campus. Students were back on campus to sign up for their next round of classes.

Kevin and Claire followed Sam's outspread arms. No matter how many times they had walked through the campus, it always managed to be quite the spectacle. It was a marvel compared to most boarding schools, as it bore a resemblance to an old medieval castle and its grounds. Originally, the grounds were meant to serve as a prestigious hotel, where the wealthy could escape on a posh vacation. It was tucked away down a long road, not far from a small town. After about a year in existence, one particularly wealthy guest, who placed a lot of value on high-level education for young adults, decided to buy the grounds and turn it into a prominent boarding academy.

Students walked along the cobblestones and through the greenery with purpose. Graduating from the Cambridge High Academy lent a certain degree of credibility to a student's resume. Everything about the school was enchanting. There was a bell tower, a few fountains, student clubhouses that served as quiet breakrooms between classes, and perhaps grandest of all, an observatory at the center of the campus.

The observatory was perhaps the most glorious structure on campus. Complete with beautifully rounded arch doorways, it looked like an ancient piece of history. The roof, which was always retracted on nice days, was a well-constructed machine. A large brass telescope sat at the center of the top floor. There were also several smaller telescopes, which the students could position at one of the many open archways on the second floor and use when the dome wasn't opened.

Everything about the Cambridge Academy campus was unique, but none of the students would ever be remembered for their fashion. Students who attended private boarding schools of this sort were required to wear a uniform—Kevin, Claire, and Sam's least favorite part of their school. They did just fine though, and it certainly made getting up and rushing out the door to class a little bit easier. Kevin and Sam had to wear khaki trousers (they were allowed khaki shorts on very hot days), blue or white Oxford shirts (which always had to be tucked in), a navy tie, and either a blazer or sweater vest. Claire's uniform was similar except for the trousers—she was to wear a khaki or navy blue pleated skirt, which was not allowed to sit higher than two inches above the knee.

The trio was already inseparable, but something was brewing that would draw them closer to one another. Kevin, after his Senior Recruitment Day failure, was determined to make the most of the rest of his Cambridge experience. The others could feel it too—there was something pulling them together. It was as real as everything that surrounded them.

"You guys feel like getting some food?" Kevin asked.

"Sure," Sam said with eager eyes.

Claire smiled. "What did you have in mind?" she asked.

"How about the main food lounge by the bell tower," Kevin said. "I heard they have a good feature sandwich today."

"Ooh," Claire said. "That sounds good. I vote we look at our class schedule too. Winter Break is over in just a couple of days and then the next semester starts. We need to be enrolled in our classes by then. Let's make sure we pick the right ones." Sam and Kevin rolled their eyes. Claire was always the prepared one of the three.

Abruptly, before the trio could even begin their usual bickering over school work, a familiar face appeared. He stood directly in front of them, smiling as if they were all already acquainted.

"Hey, you're Kevin right?" asked the familiar face.

"Hey, yeah, that's me," Kevin replied. "Greg, right? From English class?"

"Yep that's me," said Greg. "Man. I'm shocked."

Everyone paused as Greg shook his head.

"I can't believe they let complete rejects stay at Cambridge. I guess low standards are a thing here right?" Greg laughed and grabbed Kevin's shoulder. "Hey, Kev, say hello to your ex-fiancée for me, huh? Maybe she'll say yes to me—a real man." He burst into maniacal laughter.

"Grow up, you douche," Claire scoffed, pushing him off Kevin.

The rude intruder walked off just as Kevin noticed Sam clenching his fists. And as much as even Kevin wanted to retaliate, he knew he couldn't do anything but accept the truth. He avoided eye contact with Sam and Claire, hoping that they would just walk on.

"So ... sandwiches?" Claire asked. "I'm in the mood for a grilled cheese."

Kevin was glad she didn't bring up the encounter with Greg. And he also understood why. It was time for them to move on and start fresh. The only way to do that was to take it one day at a time.

※

"One grilled cheese, two feature sandwiches, and three lemon sodas," said a hefty young server, handing over a red plastic food tray packed with food.

"Thanks," Kevin, Claire, and Sam said in unison.

"Okay guys," Claire started, "I have it all mapped out. Kevin, since you're off at 1:00 on Friday and Sam is done at 2:00, I vote we designate Friday as our 'crash day.' What do you think?"

The trio had always had "crash day." It was their way of making sure they had fun together at least once a week. Whether it be a movie night or a camping trip, they made sure to always keep this time sacred. However, while their intention to set a class schedule and designate a "crash day" started off strong, their attention soon drifted. They looked over to see a group of fellow students sitting at a distant table, laughing and pointing at Kevin. Kevin began to wonder if staying at this school was a mistake.

"I just don't get it," Kevin said, frustrated. "I'm trying to move on from Susan, but how can I when everybody is constantly reminding me? This sucks."

Kevin threw his face into his hands and sighed. Both Claire and Sam stayed silent. They had no more of a clue how to deal with this than Kevin did. The silence was awkward.

Sam decided to break the silence first. "That's it," he said, getting up and adjusting his glasses. "I've had it with these guys. I'm going over there."

"Whoa there, half-pint," Claire replied and grabbed the bottom trim of Sam's sweater vest. "The last thing we need is more drama. We should simply ... ignore them. Besides, you know how the saying goes: 'Sticks and stones?'"

"Yeah, sure, I guess," Sam muttered, and sat back down. "Still would be nice to give them a piece of my mind, though."

Kevin had had enough as well. The sandwich had lost its taste, the school was no longer comfortable, and his friends were struggling to help him. He picked up his half-eaten tray of food and began to walk away ... and then he saw a girl come out of nowhere. What a pleasant sight she was. Her sparkling, emerald-green eyes were intimidating, but Kevin mustered up enough courage to nod and wave to a young lady who seemed to be taking an interest in him. Her smile was something he hadn't seen since Susan's. It complemented her rich, mahogany-brown hair, which sat in tight curls around her head. As she walked toward Kevin, her beauty prompted him to express the fondest sentiment that anyone could have, given the paralyzing circumstances.

"She's gorgeous," Kevin said out loud to himself.

"Uhh, Kevin ... Hello? Snap out of it buddy," Claire said, snapping her fingers in front of Kevin's face.

"Sorry. I was just ... yeah, never mind," Kevin said.

"We were talking about 'crash day,'" Claire said. "So ... Friday?"

"Who's gorgeous?" Sam asked.

"I uhh … umm …" Kevin said.

"Hi," said the gorgeous stranger.

Kevin was thrown off guard. He couldn't believe how charming and delicate her voice was, like silver bells ringing at Christmas time, and even more so he couldn't believe that she had come over to speak to him.

"You're Kevin, right?" the gorgeous stranger asked as she fixed her gaze on Kevin.

"Yeah," Kevin said, adjusting his tie and collar, and sitting up a little straighter.

"Sorry. I didn't mean to be weird or anything. I'm Laura. I'm a junior here too."

"Uhh … yeah, it's crazy," Kevin said. "Almost three thousand students here. Always nice to meet someone new. By the way, Laura … this is Claire and Sam."

"Nice to meet you both," Laura said, and she smiled.

"Yeah, same," Claire replied.

"Nice to meet you," Sam said, trying hard not to stare.

"I'm sorry. It's stupid, but … I just had to come and talk to you," Laura exclaimed.

"Okay. You're not here to make fun of me are you?" Kevin asked, scrunching his face up and slumping back down in his chair, as if he were about to be punched in the face.

"God, no. Absolutely not. I, umm … well I actually came to do just the opposite," said Laura, taking a brief moment to tuck her hair behind her ears. The sparkle from her earrings caught Kevin's eye. "Kevin, what you did during your scholarship speech … well … that was literally the sweetest thing I've ever seen anyone do."

"Uhh, thanks. Wow. I don't know what to say," Kevin said. His confidence rose, and so did his posture. Claire rolled her eyes as Sam beamed in delight for his friend.

"Lost for words huh? Says the bravest guy I know. That's surprising." Laura smiled again and her smile made Kevin feel warm and calm for the first time in a while. "Have you picked all your classes for the next quarter?"

"Just about. We umm ... well, we all try to pick classes that we can go to together," Kevin said looking over at his two friends.

"How cute," Laura said.

Kevin couldn't tell if she was being sincere or sarcastic. Nonetheless, he was captivated by her.

"Well," Laura said, "I'm sure you know Professor Kubo's astrology class is like, the most popular in school. It's not a required class for college, but I've heard that Kubo gives out a ton of extra credit, so it's worth our time. Maybe I'll see you there?"

"Astrology really isn't our—" Claire started.

Sam kicked her leg underneath the table, cutting off her response. She kicked back.

"Umm, yeah, sure. That sounds awesome. I'll definitely check it out," Kevin said.

"All right, great. Well ... bye, Kevin." Laura waved her dainty fingers at Kevin, her bright red nail polish catching the light.

As Laura walked away, Kevin felt alive. This feeling was reinforced by the way Sam was grinning at him.

"Wow. I can't believe it, man. I think she was really into you," Sam said. He reached across the table and gave Kevin a playful smack on his chest.

"Some of us have better things to do than to follow crushes around to classes we don't really need," Claire scoffed. "Kevin, do you even know the slightest thing about astrology?"

"Umm ... well, not really," Kevin said.

"You see. Exactly my point. Sam, would you stop encouraging him." Claire said.

"Aww come on, Claire," Sam pleaded. "Why shouldn't he? I mean, what's the worst that could happen? At the very least, he could get a ton of extra credit! Besides, this may be the best option for him to get over you know who."

"True," said Claire. "Well, I guess taking an astrology class wouldn't be so bad. I am not interested though, so I think I'll find another extracurricular class to join. Try not to drool all over your homework though."

Sam rolled his eyes at her. "What do you think, Kevin? You seriously going to join?"

"Actually ... yeah, I think I'm going to sign up," Kevin said, looking off in the direction Laura had gone.

"That-a-boy, Kevin. Looks like we're taking astrology," Sam said, and he slapped the table.

"You guys are something else," Claire said, and she shook her head.

And just like that, Kevin's fate was sealed. The forces of nature had bound him to a rollercoaster that would soon define his unique destiny. For as simple as Kubo's class may have appeared, its true depth had yet to be discovered.

☯

A couple of weeks later, Kevin and Sam were enrolled in Astrology. Kevin saw Laura in class each day, but they never seemed to get seats near each other, and so they hadn't had a chance to connect yet. Today, however, he and Sam got to class earlier than usual, and Kevin hoped this would give him the opportunity to sit next to Laura, who typically sat near the front.

Desks filled up and class started with no sign of Laura. *Maybe she is sick*, Kevin thought. He pulled out his textbook, determined to take his mind off his new crush.

"Very well, class," shouted Professor James Kubo. "It's time to open your textbooks and expand your craniums! The world is your oyster, yes. But the universe, that is your ocean."

Professor Kubo was not your typical professor. His demeanor screamed mad scientist, with a twist of proper etiquette. He had messy and unkempt grey hair that looked like it hadn't seen a pair of shears in months, but was wearing a well put-together designer suit, complete with blazer and vest. He projected a balance of perfectly organized chaos. He gestured wildly with his hands when he talked, and his voice was full of passion as he jumped from one topic to the next. Kevin could see why he made such an impression on his students.

"Now then, who can summarize chapter three for me?" asked Kubo.

Kubo's start was soon interrupted by a late student. Kevin recognized her in no time.

"Glad you could join us, Miss Laura. Please have a seat," Kubo said.

She looked around, but all the seats were taken. Kevin could see that Laura was uncomfortable—her classmates were staring at her. He looked at Laura and nodded to the empty desk to his left. This desk, in particular, stood out because it was never available. One of Cambridge's star A+ students, Beth Perkins, usually sat there—and she had never missed a day of class in her life. Normally all the front row desks would fill up as students filed in, but not Beth's desk. She took everything way too seriously, including her "regular" seat. Laura shook her head at Kevin – she didn't want to cross Beth's path, even if she was absent. She continued to look around for a better seat.

"Miss Laura," Professor Kubo was irritated. "Are you frozen in time? Class must resume—take your seat." He gestured to Beth's desk. "Miss Beth is out with the flu today, so you won't have to worry about encroaching on her territory. I won't tell her. But please, sit now."

The serendipity was uncanny. Kevin couldn't help but marvel at the lucky coincidence.

"Hey!" Laura whispered as she sat down and adjusted her t-shirt collar. Her normally tightly curled hair had been smoothed out into long, loose waves, which she tucked behind her ears and positioned.

"Hey," Kevin said.

"Hey, Laura. Cool class right?" Sam leaned over to catch her attention.

Everyone in the class paused as Kubo loudly cleared his throat and looked at Sam.

"Sorry," Sam said, leaning back and sinking further into his chair.

Kevin and Laura tried to hide their giggles as the class lecture resumed. It was Kevin's first time hearing her laugh. It was bubbly and blissful. He loved it so much that he lost focus on the blackboard's notes. All the constellations appeared as patterns of hearts and lips. Kevin was so dazed that time seemed to cease to exist. His imagination propelled him out of the classroom. Every part of his mind wandered through the cosmos as he considered whether all things in life were somehow connected. *Were Laura and I meant to meet at this very time in my life?* He wondered. Stars began to gravitate. Planets began to align. The secrets of the universe unfurled, and answers were about to be revealed. But right before he could reach for the answers he longed for, he was snapped out of his fantasy by the sound of a book being shut.

"All right everyone," said Kubo. "I expect assignment eight to be done by next week, with your work checked twice, please. If you have any questions over the weekend, you can e-mail me."

"So what do you think about the class so far?" Laura asked, turning to Kevin and Sam.

"Uhh, yeah. It's great. Just great," Kevin said. He couldn't bring himself to tell her the truth about what he was actually paying attention to.

"I know, right?" Laura said raising her eyebrows in excitement. "I told you. Kubo is amazing, isn't he? It's like he takes astrology to a whole new level."

"Yeah, he definitely does," Kevin said.

"So I guess I'll see you next week?" Laura said, looking at Sam and Kevin.

"Yep. Definitely," Kevin said, adjusting his tie.

"Great. Bye, Kevin. Bye, Sam."

"Bye Laura." They both waved as she ventured off.

"God, she's really something isn't she, Sam?" Kevin sighed as he stood up from his desk.

"She's something all right. So, when are you going to ask her out?" Sam asked.

"I don't know. I'm still getting over Susan, you know," Kevin said reluctantly.

"Come on, Kevin. What could there possibly be to think about? Claire and I both think she's cool. I say just go for it. She clearly likes you." Sam playfully tapped Kevin in the chest.

"Yeah, maybe I'll—" Kevin started to say before he was interrupted by an unexpected force that knocked him and his books over. As quickly as he could, he bent down to pick up his papers and books, which were scattered like his feelings. He looked up and saw Professor Kubo doing the same thing.

"I'm so sorry, Professor Kubo. I didn't mean to," Kevin said.

"Nonsense, Mr. Deer. It's all my fault. Really," Kubo said.

They picked up the last bit of academic papers they each had dropped.

"There now, you see? No harm done," Kubo said. "You boys study hard this weekend. Remember ... the universe is your ocean."

Kevin and Sam nodded, embarrassed they had blindsided their professor, and quickly walked away.

"Geez, Kevin," Sam said. "Hope he doesn't give us an incomplete in his class now."

Kevin laughed and gave Sam a friendly shove. They both looked up to see Claire waiting for them in the hallway with her books nestled in her arms. She smiled her usual warm and inviting smile, and her coffee-brown eyes glistened in the hallway light.

"What's wrong with you?" Kevin asked Sam. He noticed that Sam's face was flushed more than usual.

"Nothing," Sam said, looking down.

"Hey, you two. How's astrology going?" Claire asked.

"It was going great until Kevin decided to get us flunked from the class," Sam teased.

"Wait, what?" Claire asked.

"Uhh, long story. He's joking," Kevin said, shaking his head.

"Weirdos," Claire muttered.

"Hey so are we still on for crash day later on?" Kevin asked.

"Sure," Claire replied. "What did you have in mind?"

"Well, Sam and I have an astrology assignment due next week, and we were thinking of studying at the observatory," Kevin said. "It could be fun. We can bring some snacks and camp out."

"Hmm … spending my Friday night studying with you two knuckleheads?" Claire paused and thought over Kevin's proposal. "Okay, wouldn't miss it for the world. You'll bring the popcorn?"

"Uhh, that's Sam's job," Kevin said.

"Why is it always my job to get popcorn now?" asked Sam begrudgingly.

"I don't know … maybe because you always finish it all," Kevin said.

Everyone laughed. It was starting to feel like old times again. For the first time since senior recruitment day, Kevin felt a sense of relief. Things were looking up. His friends, Laura,

Cambridge, it was all making sense now. *My stars are aligning,* he thought to himself.

✧

Kevin reached down into the brown bag and stuffed his face with another handful of popcorn. He made room for Claire, who wanted to grab her share before Sam noticed the half-eaten bag. The three were in the observatory to officially start "crash day." It was a clear night, so the observatory had opened its dome and set the smaller telescopes out, pointing toward the open sky. The stars aligned that night with the celestial patterns of romance.

"You okay over there, Sam?" Kevin asked.

"Yeah. Just trying to figure out which one is Ursa Major," Sam replied, as he smoothed out his astrology chart and toyed with one of the smaller telescopes.

Kevin and Claire shook their heads and smiled. They decided to let their friend have his fun while they peered over the balcony of the elegant and modern observatory tower. The large brass telescope was pointed toward the center of the sky, ready to share the universe's secrets with the next student to cross its path. There were no boundaries here, just the observers and the beautiful governing concepts of space.

"So, things are going well with you and Laura?" Claire asked.

"Yeah, I guess, we haven't talked much. Sam thinks she likes me," Kevin said.

"What do you think?" Claire asked. She braced herself for the truth.

"I don't know. I mean you know it's been really hard to get over Susan," Kevin said.

"Yeah, I know," Claire said.

"I guess part of me has hope that I could fall in love with Laura. You know? Why not?" Kevin said.

"How do you do it?" Claire asked.

"What do you mean?" Kevin said confused.

"I mean, this. This situation," Claire said. "How do you keep going? After everything that Susan did to you, how do you put yourself out there again? I feel like anyone else would be scared to keep believing in love after that."

"Hmm," Kevin paused, running his hands through his hair and shaking it out. "You know, I don't know," he said. "I guess it's just a bit of faith. And maybe a bit of foolishness. You know when I was giving that speech, I really meant every word. I guess, well, before my parents died ... I knew how much magic they had in the love they shared. It was pure and real. I'd give anything to have that. And I truly believe that if you put positive energy out there, you will receive something positive in return."

Claire looked at Kevin and smiled. "You're a good guy, Kevin."

"And what about you? Do you believe in love?" Kevin asked.

Claire put her head down and picked at her cuticles. "Well, you know my parents split up a while back," she said. "I guess I never really believed much in love after that. I mean, I guess the only people I consider my real family are you and Sam." Claire looked back at Kevin and shrugged.

Kevin smirked.

"What?" Claire asked.

"Nothing," said Kevin.

"Tell me." Claire poked Kevin in the chest.

Kevin conceded. "It's just that … well, I think you probably believe in love more than you think. Just because you're afraid of it, doesn't mean it doesn't exist. And it certainly doesn't mean you shouldn't believe in it.

"Do you believe that things happen for a reason, Claire? I do. I mean, you have to. Look at us—what pulled us together to become friends? You and I and Sam … we're all different people. Like, completely different. But there's something about each of us that belongs to the other person—it's like we are each other's missing pieces. I think that's the most real definition of fate that I can think of. We were destined to be friends."

"Maybe you're right," Claire said.

It was Claire's first time being surprised by her friend. Kevin had known her for years, and for him to know something about her that she herself didn't know made it all the more obvious why they were such good friends. The feeling made her heart flutter. She decided to throw some popcorn at him to change the subject.

"Umm … Hey, guys!" Sam shouted from across the way. "You're not going to believe what I just found."

"Let's go check out what he's talking about, lover boy," Claire said.

"Nice," Kevin said as he brushed popcorn from his jacket. "You're a real comedian."

"Come on." Claire pulled Kevin's arm.

The two friends walked over to Sam, who looked puzzled as he frantically flipped through pages of a textbook.

"Guys, this isn't Kevin's book," Sam said, tapping at the pages.

"What do you mean?" Kevin asked. "I've had it all day since astrology."

"Exactly," Sam said. "This is *Kubo's* book. I think you might have grabbed it by mistake when you guys bumped into each other. Look." Sam held the open pages inches away from Kevin and Claire's faces.

Kevin, Claire, and Sam marveled at the meticulous notes inside the book. Every single page was covered with sticky notes, intricate scribbles, and taped loose notepad pages. Almost every page was yellow and cracked, as if it had been slowly decomposing for hundreds of years. Medieval-looking art occupied space every few pages—designs of women with crazy hair, and no faces. A Zodiac sign and descriptions accompanied each woman's picture. It was an odd book. It felt as heavy as a rock—as if it were packed with obscure secrets.

"You're right," Kevin said. He traced a drawing of an Aries with his fingers. "This isn't my book. It must be Kubo's!"

Kevin flipped through some more pages then laid the book on the table in front of them. It automatically fell open to a page titled, "The Mistresses of the Zodiac." The book fell so easily to this page, it was as if Kevin had been meant to find it.

"What are the 'Twelve Mistresses of the Zodiac?'" Claire asked, confused, as she read a few inserts. "It says here that 'the zodiac brings you true love.' What does that mean?"

Kevin took the book off the table and pored over each note. "Guys, I don't think this is a textbook for *any* of the classes here."

"It's not?" asked Claire.

"It can't be. There's not even an author," Kevin said. "It also looks like Kubo may have even written some of the content himself. And who knows who did these drawings—they look hand-sketched."

"Maybe it's just a research book," Claire said and shrugged.

"I'm not so sure about that," Kevin said. As he continued to flip through the pages, an old, yellow envelope fell to the ground from the last page of the book.

The three friends looked at one another. "Where did that come from?" Sam asked. "We've been flipping through this book for at least five minutes now … how come we didn't see this letter?"

Kevin bent down to pick it up.

☾

Claire and Sam looked in anticipation as Kevin carefully opened the envelope. Although it was just an envelope, it was unlike anything modern. It looked to be hundreds of years old, and it was made of thick stock, as if it had importance lined into it. What was even more important than the envelope however, were its contents.

Kevin pulled out an old, thick parchment that was folded into three equal portions. He carefully unfolded it, making sure to not further rip or damage the weathered paper. It looked even older than the envelope and had the same medieval art from inside the book inscribed onto it. Kevin read out loud what was written in an old-fashioned English script and ink.

> **"May the universe become the ocean of opportunity to all who embark on this quest,**
> **True love is simply a year away for any who are brave enough to take its test.**
> **And as the seasons turn and love bares to more than one soul,**
> **The Spirits of the Zodiac have indeed chosen to bring about love's role.**
> **Aries, Taurus, Gemini, Cancer, Leo, Virgo, Libra, Scorpio, Sagittarius**
> **Capricorn, Aquarius, and Pisces, you are all the Zodiac. This you must trust.**

Just as Kevin finished reading, a few of the letters began to mysteriously glow.

"This feels a little weird guys," Claire said, her tone signaling she was unsure about their doings. "I vote we give Kubo his book back."

"Come on, Claire. It's not weird—it's kind of neat," Sam replied. "Maybe it was written with disappearing ink or something."

"Maybe … Wait, what's that?" Claire said, as she pointed to the back of the parchment. "Was that there before? I swear I just saw some gold flourishes appear on the page."

Kevin quickly turned the letter around and put the piece of paper down.

Sam frowned. "I don't see anything, Claire."

"No, no, something was happening." Claire picked the letter back up and began to wave the piece of paper around. "C'mon letter—start writing again!"

"Claire! Be gentle—you could rip it!" Kevin reached for the letter. As he grabbed the letter from Claire, he waved it under a beam of moonlight and he caught a glimpse of gold glitter. "Wait! Claire, I saw it! The gold writing."

Kevin held the letter up to the moonlight and he, Claire, and Sam stared in awe as a secret message appeared, written in gold ink. It could only be seen when held to the light, and it sparkled as Kevin read it out loud:

"In order for anyone to find true love, one must consider the following rules:

- The enchanted path shall begin as soon as one inscribes their name with ink.

- During each phase of a Zodiac sign, a mister or mistress whose sign matches the phase of that time shall inevitably cross your path. You'll have the time of that Zodiac phase to discover love with that sign.

- The Zodiac sign of each phase must confess their love in either spoken word or writing, and each confession must be witnessed by two or more souls.

- Once each mister or mistress proclaims their love, a choice to accept or move on shall follow. You may choose to love, however this will not be your true love, and it will not last.

- Once all twelve Zodiac signs have confessed their love within the twelve month calendar year, a thirteenth opportunity shall emerge.
- If one is able to complete this feat, the thirteenth mister or mistress whom you love, and who loves you in return, will be your true love for life.

BEWARE: ONE WHO FAILS OR STOPS THIS QUEST WILL LOSE TRUE LOVE FOREVER

"Is that Kubo's signature?" Claire asked.

Kevin and Sam looked to where she pointed. She was right. Among dozens of signatures, Kubo's was the last that blessed the bottom of the parchment.

This moment represented the most profound silence any of them had ever experienced. Given the series of events that had led up to this point, it was quite obvious what each one of them was thinking. All attention turned to Kevin.

"Guys, you know what this means, right?" Sam asked. His eyes were bright with life.

"What? That we should give Kubo his book back and pretend we didn't read any of this weirdness?" Claire said snarkily.

In most cases, Claire was optimistic and encouraging of a good adventure. But this was different. Her feelings for Kevin were too powerful to just let go. She felt that if Kevin did find his true *'love for life'* as the parchment promised, she would lose him. Just thinking of it made her stomach tighten. She couldn't imagine having to watch it unfold in front of her.

"Umm, no. It means we finally found how you can find love again," Sam said, looking at Kevin. "It means we *have* to do this." Sam grabbed the letter from Kevin and pulled a pen out of his pocket. He placed the letter on the table in front of them and held the pen out, waving it in front of Kevin's face.

Sam had his own selfish motivations as well. He couldn't help but imagine a couple of possible outcomes to this. The first would be that maybe Claire would finally believe in love and give him a chance. The second was that if this worked for Kevin, then he would do it himself—with the intention of having Claire be his thirteenth love.

"Wait? Are you serious?" squawked Claire. "This is clearly a joke, Sam. Ugh. Why am I the only sensible one? Kevin, would you please talk him out of this?"

"No, he's right," Kevin said, staring off. His blue eyes sparkled in the moonlight; he had a sense of renewed excitement. "He's absolutely right."

"You can't be serious," Claire said.

"Think about it," Kevin said. "Everything happens for a reason right? I mean, what if Susan leaving me was so that I could eventually find *real* love? Or even find her again? Because of Susan, I met Laura. And what if meeting Laura was meant to lead me to this? Without Laura, I wouldn't have joined Kubo's class. Then I wouldn't have run into him and now found this letter. Yes, it could be a stupid prank. But what if it isn't? What if this was all meant to be? Us at this observatory, looking at the stars, finding this parchment. You just asked me *how do I do it*, Claire. This is it. It takes a leap of faith, so I won't ever regret taking that leap. I know there's something out there. I just know."

Claire took a moment to let everything sink in. Kevin's face showed nothing but dignity. Sam shrugged his shoulders. They were all on the verge of embarking on something quite phenomenal. Despite her personal bias, she couldn't bring herself to discourage her friend. This could be just what he needed to get over Susan, and Claire would consider that a victory in itself.

"Okay, I'm on board. So what now?" Claire asked.

"We should make a pact," Sam said.

"A pact?" Claire asked.

"Yeah. It'll be just like our first camping trip. To help him out with this. That's what friends are for, right?"

"Yeah." Claire smiled.

"You guys don't have to—" Kevin began.

"Enough, lover boy," Claire said, holding her hand up to Kevin's face. "We're in. We're a trio. Besides, this could be a lot of fun. Not sure I agree with the whole 'breaking-hearts' thing, but ... if it's just helping you get a date or two, then I see nothing wrong with that."

Sam placed his pen down on the table next to the letter. Kevin picked it up and paused for a second.

What if this was true? Kevin thought. *Was the risk of losing love forever worth the attempt to find it?*

"There," Kevin said as he signed his name in big cursive letters. The black ink dried gold, and as Kevin traced his name on the letter, he noticed that it felt like it had been embossed onto the page. "So that's it? We're really doing this?"

"You bet," Claire replied.

"Yes!" Sam shouted, pumping his first in the air. "But, we have to agree that this is our secret. We won't tell anybody about what we found or what we're doing. Agreed?" Sam looked over at Claire and Kevin, who both nodded silently.

"Okay then, guys. On the count of three ... One, two ..." Sam gave his friends a chance to bring their fists in to his.

"Three!" they chimed in unison and threw their hands up.

And so it was. Kevin and his friends had sealed the start of their new adventure with a pact. Their journey to find true love through 'The Twelve Mistresses of the Zodiac' had begun.

❧

"Okay so I was thinking," Sam said as he and Kevin walked to Astrology class the following Monday. "It's going to be hard to just randomly pick out a girl that happens to be an Aries, let alone one that could potentially love you. We may have a better shot looking at a dating site."

"I am not getting on a dating site," Kevin said forcefully. "Besides, I believe in fate. It should just happen, right? If the universe wants me to find love, it will provide me with the tools to do just that."

"Yeah well, I hate to be your dose of reality here but ... you only have a week until the Aries phase starts," Sam said.

"Yeah, who knows, right?" Kevin said. "Maybe this is impossible. But I've got to try. The stars will align, trust me."

Kevin and Sam walked into their classroom and anticipated that Kubo would immediately ask for his book back. They had worked all morning to reseal the envelope and organize his notes back to normal as best as they could. Kevin hoped they wouldn't get in trouble for this invasion of privacy. He would hate to lose this class. And as he spotted Laura in her usual seat, it occurred to him that he would hate even more to lose his opportunity with her.

"Hello everyone. Please take your seats," said a tall stranger.

Kevin and Sam were thrown off by this unfamiliar face.

"Now I know it's a bit of a surprise to see me. I'm Mr. Thompson—your stand-in teacher for this class. Unfortunately, Professor Kubo …" Thompson paused. "Unfortunately, Professor Kubo has passed away. It was reported to the staff over the weekend. I know Professor Kubo was very well regarded by every one of you. I shall do my very best to fill his shoes during the remainder of this semester."

There was total silence. A combination of shock and disbelief swept through the room. Students looked over at one another, hoping somebody in the class would know what had happened. They were all met with the same confused looks.

"Very well, then …" Thompson continued. "If you would please take your textbooks out and turn to page fifty-seven …"

Kevin looked at Sam, who shrugged and whispered, "Let's not worry about it."

"*Psst* … Hey Kevin," whispered Laura.

"Hey," Kevin said.

"How awful about Kubo right?" Laura said. "I feel so sad. He was becoming one of my favorite teachers here."

"Yeah. It's strange actually …" Kevin said, stopping because he knew he couldn't explain why he thought it was so strange. How would he tell Laura about his night with Claire and Sam in the observatory over the weekend? Where would he even begin? Luckily, Laura kept talking.

"It sucks," Laura said. "I had planned on inviting a bunch of people from class to a party next weekend. It's spring break and my parents are out of town for the whole week, so I figured it was perfect timing for us to have some fun. But now I'm not so sure. Everyone may be a bit preoccupied." Laura handed Kevin one of her invitations.

"Maybe a party is what everyone needs to cheer up," Kevin suggested.

"Yeah, maybe you're right," Laura replied with hope. "Well, you and your friends should come. Her green eyes glittered as she said flirtatiously to Kevin, "It would be really fun to have *you* there specifically." She turned back to taking notes and bit the top of her pencil, too nervous to see Kevin's reaction to what she'd said.

Kevin couldn't believe his eyes when he looked down at her invitation. He passed it to Sam, who looked just as stunned. This was no ordinary spring break party. It was Laura's birthday party. Laura was an Aries.

CHAPTER II

—THE ARIES WITH AN APPETITE FOR ANGER —

Aries: March 21ˢᵗ—April 19ᵗʰ

The Aries, a noble fire sign, is often seen as independent and passionate but can prove to be quite the handful. The Aries loves to take risks and often maintains a childlike innocence as part of their independent nature. With passion leading their lives, they will protect their friends and family, at any expense. While these traits allow the Aries to provide for a life full of exciting adventure, it is their dark side that is often forgotten. Such strong passion often leads the Aries down the path of extreme stubbornness and anger. The Aries mistress does not like to be asked to wait and will not tolerate being scorned. When placed in the heat of the moment, the Aries will not back down. For Kevin and his friends, will they recognize these traits too late?

Claire pushed her sandwich away as Kevin and Sam walked up. It had been a few days since they all had discovered the mysterious parchment in Kubo's book, but it seemed like the stars were already aligning. Kevin felt hopeful that he was on the right track.

"So how did it go when you gave Kubo his book back?" Claire asked.

"Umm, yeah. So the thing is—"Kevin began.

"What? Oh no, Kevin. Please don't tell me you guys got kicked out of his class for this? This isn't worth it," Claire said as she put her hand over her forehead in dismay.

"No. No. It's not that. Actually, Kubo wasn't there," Kevin said.

"What do you mean 'Kubo wasn't there?'" Claire asked, squinting her eyes in confusion.

"He wasn't there," Sam reiterated.

"So he's like, sick or something?" Claire asked.

"Actually, he died," Kevin replied.

"What!" Claire said. She covered her mouth with her hands. "Are you kidding? You don't find that the least bit weird and too coincidental? That's horrible!"

"Claire, you're blowing things out of proportion," Sam exclaimed. "People die. It's life."

"It's not something to take lightly, Sam," Claire said, frowning. "How do we know this wasn't connected? This is a book that we are using to find Kevin his one true love and we made him sign a mysterious letter. Here, let me see the book."

Kevin yielded as Claire grabbed the book from him. He was impressed by how quickly she sifted through the pages. And even though he wished she was a bit more optimistic, he was grateful for her protective instinct and rationality.

"Okay. Look," Claire said, pointing at the handwritten text. "Right here. Aries is the first mistress you need to find right? Well, it's the next cycle to come if we were to do this. Look at this."

Kevin and Sam both looked at the page Claire had discovered. The page titled *Aries* had a hand-drawn illustration of a faceless woman with sketched ram horns added into her hair. But what was more interesting was what the text said:

"The Aries Mistress—a sign who lives from March 21st through April 19th.
The allure of the Aries mistress is genuine. It is real.
One should be thought lucky to be within her appeal.
But beware, those who are within the midst of an Aries stranger,
should consider wisely, for on this quest, one could unravel anger."

"What's that mean?" Sam asked.

"The Aries gets upset. But everyone does, right?" Kevin replied.

"Yeah, that's true. But why would that be the mistresses' emphasis?" Claire asked. "There's got to be something to this. Kubo wouldn't have written it down if it wasn't an important connection. What if this book is how Kubo died, guys? I think we should tread carefully until we figure out what this all really means."

Kevin and Sam were quiet but looked at each other as if they were hiding a secret.

"What?" Claire asked as she scowled at them.

Kevin gave in first. "Okay," he said, pulling on his left ear nervously. "So we *may* have gotten an invitation to go to Laura's birthday party next week. And she just might be an Aries. Well, no, she *is* an Aries."

"This is so not a good idea," Claire said, rolling her eyes.

"So what are you saying?" Sam demanded of Claire. "That just because she's an Aries she's an angry person? That can't be true. Laura's super nice. Why else would she invite us to her party? I'm pretty sure Kevin isn't going to die from having fun at a party."

"Look," Claire said. "I'm not saying that, all right? My mom is an Aries, and she's the sweetest woman I know. Me, I'm a Scorpio. I don't necessarily feel like I fit the stereotypical Zodiac descriptions and predictions of a Scorpio. I'm just saying that we should be careful. This whole thing could have unexpected consequences."

"You're a Scorpio?" Sam asked. "Cool." He wondered how they paired with Cancers.

"Yes, Sam," Claire said. "I'm a Scorpio, you are a Cancer, and Kevin is a Libra. Is that all you got from what I was saying? Geez. Why am I the only sensible one?"

"Look," Kevin said, "I get that this could get weird, but we don't even know if it's real or not. We made a pact. For now, let's just see how it goes." He hoped to remove the frown from Claire's face; he was worried the wrinkles in her forehead would start to stick.

"Okay fine," Claire said. "But the minute this gets too weird, we're getting rid of Kubo's book."

"Agreed," Kevin and Sam said in unison.

ᘒ

The Intro to Astrology class was less crowded than usual, and no one seemed to be paying attention. Kubo's unfortunate absence was completely apparent as Professor Thompson focused on bathing the blackboard with dull scribbles and doodles. He lacked the passion that Kubo brought to the class. Kevin, who seldom paid attention to anything but Laura, also found Thompson less interesting than his predecessor, and so continued to direct his focus to his beautiful classmate.

"So as you see, the constellation Orion would actually be centered along this region," Professor Thompson explained.

"Umm … Excuse me, professor?" Laura asked raising her hand.

"Yes?" Thompson asked.

"We had already gone over this chapter with Professor Kubo," Laura said.

"I understand," Thompson said. "Please forgive the inconvenience of all this. However, I'm quite sure a refresher won't hurt. More important, I expect all of my students to be experts on this material, given the refresher course. You'll be quizzed on it."

"You're kidding right?" Laura asked. She was getting flustered, and her face was turning red. "Why on earth would we have to repeat something we've already learned? It seems like a waste of time, if you ask me."

"I beg your pardon," Thompson said shocked. "You are out of line. As a professor here I—"

"If you were a real professor, you'd have your act together wouldn't you?" Laura scoffed.

"Miss, I am very close to giving you a failing grade in this class," Thompson said, his hands on his hips now.

"Screw you!" Laura said, her voice considerably louder than before.

"Enough!" Thompson said.

Laura slammed her fists on her desk. Even Professor Thompson was thrown off by her outburst, and everyone did their best not to make eye contact with the frustrated young student.

Kevin and Sam had even more reason for concern. They were thinking about Kubo's book and the description of the Aries mistress that Claire had read to them. Kevin, whose feelings for Laura had already grown stronger now, decided to ignore the outburst and brush it off as a simple coincidence, unrelated to her zodiac sign.

"Hey. You okay?" Kevin whispered, softly resting his hand on Laura's arm.

Laura looked at him with appreciation. It was clear she was upset.

"Yeah, I'm sorry for that. I'm just stressed out about my party tonight. I have a lot left to do to get the house ready. You're still coming, right?" Laura whispered.

"Of course," Kevin replied. "We wouldn't miss it for the world."

"Good. Because I really want to see you there." Laura smiled and rested her hand on top of Kevin's, giving it a quick squeeze.

Kevin's heart leaped. "Me too," he said.

"Here's my number," Laura said, as she slipped Kevin a small note. "Text me okay?"

Kevin looked at Sam, who had an awkward and nervous smile on his face.

"After class. We need to talk," Sam mouthed to Kevin.

Kevin nodded. He knew what Sam was concerned about. For now he just wanted to ignore it. This was his first interaction with someone special since Susan, and he had every intention of savoring it. The daydreams resumed. The blackboard turned into a dreamy watercolor of a starry sky. Voices were muted. All he could hear was his heart beating. It was perfect.

The next thing he heard was Thompson saying, "Class dismissed." Thompson began erasing the blackboard and then turned back to face the class, and giving Laura a hard stare, said, "Oh, and … I expect everyone to be ready for the pop quiz next week on Orion."

Laura rolled her eyes and turned her attention back to Kevin.

"I have to run to pick up some things for the party, but I'll see you guys tonight okay?"

"Absolutely," Kevin said. He smiled back at her, and she walked out of class. Once she disappeared into the halls, he snapped out of his fantasy to the sound of students gathering their books in anticipation for the weekend. Laura often had that effect on him. Tonight, at her party, he planned to muster up the the courage to ask her out.

"Do me a favor, will you?" Kevin asked Sam.

"Sure," Sam said.

"Don't tell Claire about Laura getting upset in class today," Kevin said.

"Why?" Sam asked.

"Just trust me," Kevin said. "Can I count on you?"

"Yeah, I guess, Sam said. "But—"

"No 'buts,'" Kevin said. "I need this. I don't want Claire to worry unless there's really a reason for it."

Sam lowered his head in resignation. It wasn't like them to keep secrets from each other like this. On top of that, Sam felt this was a legitimate issue. If this was some kind of omen and Laura was truly a stereotypical Aries whose behavior could turn into something bad, it would certainly not be the smartest idea to ignore the problem. But Sam nodded to let Kevin know he understood and would keep quiet.

❧

Claire had been sitting in the dimly lit library for hours now. Under normal circumstances, she wouldn't skip class for anything. In this case, however, she felt justified. The computer screen was spitting out information, yet none of it gave her any specific clues pertaining to Kubo. Claire was getting frustrated and her contacts were stinging inside her eyes. She had been staring at the screen for too long. She rubbed her eyes to bring them back to life and twisted her smooth, black hair back into a bun and secured it with a pencil. Then she resumed clicking and scrolling. Other than a few articles announcing Kubo's death (none of which provided any clues as to why or how he died) and a few on his most recent academic achievements, there wasn't much information. She wondered if her concerns were indeed unfounded, and hated the idea of her friends, especially Kevin, spending time on something that could be a dead end. *Maybe Kubo was just writing a clever fiction book?* Claire thought. She shook her head, determined to find an answer. She had a very strong hunch there was something to this, so she kept searching.

"Bingo," Claire muttered.

There it was. She had found an article about Kubo and his excursions to some of the most remote regions of the world. It was clear he had accumulated a vast amount of knowledge on his travels. The article reported that Kubo was eager to learn whether the Zodiac signs were respected in other countries and if so, study how those countries let those beliefs guide their own individual understanding of love. The more pressing matter was whether any of this knowledge would explain the mysterious book and envelope they had discovered. She typed "The 12 Mistresses of the Zodiac" into the search bar of her webpage in hopes of finding more information. Multiple articles by Kubo popped up.

"How to Find Your Perfect Zodiac Match"

"Zodiac Personality Traits"

"In-Depth Studies of Astrology"

"How Other Cultures View the Zodiac"

She clicked on each of them, but none of them were what she was looking for. It was pointless. But just when she'd decided to pack up her things and quit, she uncovered something meaningful: "The 12 Mistresses of the Zodiac" by James Kubo, PhD.

She clicked the link, and immediately a PDF file downloaded to her computer. She was glad that she'd trusted her gut to keep searching, because it now appeared that she'd been right to believe that there was something to the other night. The PDF was a dissertation located on a hidden site. Whoever hosted this file did not want this information to be found very easily.

It was at that moment that Claire knew. "This could actually be true," she whispered to herself.

She felt goosebumps on her arms, and a feeling of dread sank in. It crept over her like an icy chill, and she felt numb for a second. Almost as if her body knew she had discovered something she shouldn't have. She looked around, but her attention was immediately drawn back to her computer when she heard a "bing."

A blue light had appeared on the computer screen. It was the school's general messenger alert. Claire was puzzled. She had never used it before and wondered who it could be as she opened it up.

"WELCOME TO CAMBRIDGE MESSENGER. YOU HAVE 1 NEW MESSAGE FROM {Z}. Would you like to accept?"

She clicked on 'yes,' and waited for the prompt.

   · *Hi...*
Z at 3:12pm
   · *Hi....who is this??*
Claire at 3:12pm

> · *It does not matter. What matters is that I know what you are doing.*
>
> Z at 3:13pm

More chills ran down Claire's spine. She looked around the empty library to see if anyone was playing a prank on her. She saw a student in a trucker hat sound asleep on a nearby couch—clearly not the culprit. She and Z must have been the only two people in that study hall on a computer; she grew even more concerned.

> · *You and your friends should be careful when playing with matters of the heart. Tonight, you will see why :-)*
>
> Z at 3:15pm

That was it. Claire had enough. She e-mailed the dissertation to herself, signed out of the messenger program, shut the computer off, and gathered her bag. She gave another quick glance to her sleeping library neighbor, just to be sure he wasn't the culprit. He wasn't. Claire gripped her bag tighter. She couldn't remember the last time she'd been this scared. She had good reason; Z's threat had mentioned "tonight." All she could do was hope that she and her friends weren't in over their heads. Tonight, at Laura's party, she would be sure to keep a lookout.

꙾

Sam relaxed on his dorm room bed and gazed at the ceiling. The stale furniture made daydreams more vivid. He tried to imagine the ceiling as the astrology chart from class, and figure out where his place was in the wide universe. Until now, he had always viewed the stars as something mundane. But recent events were making him wonder just how deeply the cosmos and universe were connected to the human race.

"Man, I can't believe you were lucky enough to not have roommates," Kevin shouted from the bathroom.

"Yeah. It's cool, I guess," Sam said. "Hey, are you almost done? Do you think it will make a bad impression if we show up late?"

"I wouldn't worry about it," Kevin said. "I got a text back from Laura. She said the party is just starting now. We'll be fine."

Sam's worry was still present. He wondered if Laura would get upset if they showed up late. He knew her outburst from earlier wasn't normal but had no idea how to communicate the situation to Kevin. It was clear that Kevin liked her, and telling him could cause a rift between the two friends. After everything that had transpired with Susan, it was the last thing Sam wanted to do to his friend. He decided to get in the party spirit and put some music on from his computer.

"Any special music requests?" Sam yelled.

"Nah, man. Knock yourself out. I'm almost finished," Kevin shouted.

Sam took the permission to heart and decided to play his favorite hits, which were fast-paced beats with no real rhythm. He liked it despite how unpopular it was and often found himself bobbing his head to the beat, as he was doing now.

"I take it back. Anything but this," Kevin yelled.

Sam laughed. He decided to tease Kevin by turning up the volume but was interrupted by a blue pop-up screen. Sam had received a Cambridge Messenger notification. He grew excited, hoping it was one of the girls from across the hall, and clicked it open.

> · Hi!
> Z at 5:12pm

"Hmm. I don't know any Z's," Sam muttered.

> · Hey!! Do I know you?
> Sam at 5:12pm

> · It does not matter. What matters is that I know what you are doing.
> Z at 5:13pm

"That's kind of weird," Sam said to himself. Inexperienced when it came to social norms, he assumed this was the new way of flirting. He decided to play along.

> · That's super hot…
> Sam at 5:14pm

Then he shook his head in embarrassment. "Super hot? What are you thinking, Sam? That's not cute."

> · You and your friends will find out soon enough. For now, enjoy your Zodiac journey. Watch your back. Consider yourself warned.
> Z at 5:15pm

Sam froze.

"Hey man. What happened to the music?" said Kevin. He was now standing near Sam and had finished buttoning up his shirt.

Before Sam could answer, there was a knock on the door. Sam turned his laptop screen to black and proceeded to the door with caution. He looked back at Kevin, who had a puzzled expression on his face, and signaled him to keep quiet.

"Claire?" Sam asked when he opened the door.

Claire gave him a frown. "Yeah. Were you expecting someone else?"

"Not exactly," Sam said, scratching his head.

"I gotta say, between the two of you, I don't know who's weirder," Claire teased. "Whoa. Look at you, Casanova. Someone is definitely trying to dress to impress."

Claire was taken aback. She had never seen Kevin so fashionable. He had on a dark blue long-sleeved button-down dress shirt, paired with slim jeans and beautiful dark brown leather dress shoes. Part of her was happy to see him getting out, while another part of her wished he wasn't going and was instead taking her out on a date.

"Aww, come on," Kevin said, embarrassed, pulling at his sleeve cuffs.

"So are we leaving now?" Claire asked. "I overheard some people leaving here saying that it's getting kind of crowded."

"I'm ready if you guys are," Kevin said.

"What about you, doorman?" Claire said, teasing Sam, who was still holding the door open. She paused when she realized her joke had fallen flat. Sam's eyes were wide as he stared down at the floor, deep in thought. "Hey, are you okay? You look like you've seen a ghost."

"Yeah. I'm fine," Sam said. He shook his head and walked back to his computer.

Everyone looked over at Sam's computer screen as a beeping alerted Sam to a new message.

"Who's that?" Claire asked. She frowned as if she knew Sam was hiding something.

"No one," Sam said. "Just somebody who may be at the party later." He couldn't bring himself to spoil Kevin's big night.

Claire's frown stuck. She wasn't buying it.

"That's awesome, man. Guess we should get going then?" Kevin said.

"Sure," Claire said, trying to figure out why Sam was acting so strange.

Sam turned his computer off as they headed out the door. He was spooked. He decided to wait until after the party to tell the others about the message he'd received. He hoped that this was just a random, poorly timed prank.

"Hey, guys. Wait up," Sam said, jogging behind Claire and Kevin.

The three friends walked down the hallway and out of the Cambridge dorms. The sound of the wind rushing over the trees gave the night an eerie feeling.

❧

The night was young and alive. The scent of mowed grass and the sound of music filled the air as Kevin, Claire, and Sam walked across the front yard and up to the door of Laura's house. Their first house party was starting off nothing short of exhilarating.

Kevin took the lead and opened the front door. Inside, the party was so crowded that they needed to elbow and shove their way through to get anywhere. The unidentified music was now revealed to have two sources—a DJ booth inside and a live rock band outside. The two clashed with each other, but there was enough alcohol that people didn't seem to mind as they danced aimlessly through the house. It was a maze anybody would enjoy getting lost in.

"I'm going to try and find Laura," Kevin shouted over the music.

He gave a thumbs-up as Claire and Sam nodded and proceeded into the euphoric mass of jumbled students. Kevin looked at his phone to see if he had received anything. He had. He smiled as he clicked open a text from Laura.

> From Laura at 9:27 pm: Hey you! When you get here, come find me near the live band. I'll be in front with something special on for you ;-)

Kevin decided to follow the faint sound of the live band, knowing she would be there as promised. Kevin glided through the house until he was summoned out of his trance by an unfamiliar presence.

"You must be Kevin," said the stranger, touching his arm.

"I'm sorry. Do I know you?" Kevin said with disappointment. Whoever she was, she wasn't Laura.

"Sorry. I just … I know you through Laura. Well kind of. I may have looked you up on social media after she mentioned you," the stranger giggled. "My name's Gracie," She extended her right hand while pushing her bangs aside with her left. She had icy gray eyes that sparkled in contrast to her jet black hair.

"Uhh, cool," Kevin replied, shaking Gracie's hand quickly. "Umm … have you seen Laura? I kind of told her I'd meet her near the band." He looked around, showing no interest in continuing a conversation with Gracie.

"Oh yeah. Just right out that way," Gracie said, pointing

toward the entrance to the back yard. "I just love bands. This one in particular. You know, I heard that Laura's old dorm-mate Libby had the biggest crush on the lead singer. But then, he broke Libby's heart when he ..."

Kevin didn't care to decipher all of Gracie's chattering over the loud music. All he cared about was getting to Laura.

"Look, umm ... I don't mean to be rude. I'm going to go find Laura," Kevin said, shouting to be heard over the commotion. He ignored any further attempts at chatter and walked quickly toward the music. Ordinarily, he would have loved to make the acquaintance of someone new, but the prospect of seeing Laura was too urgent.

The outside area was much calmer than inside, and the band was playing a mellow tune. It was soothing. However, Kevin only had one thing on his mind. He finally spotted Laura— she was wearing an "I love astrology" t-shirt, tucked into high waisted denim shorts that had a number of small carefully placed rips in them. All he could do was take in the moment.

"Kevin!" Laura said signaling him with a wave. "Over here."

Kevin pushed through the slight crowd. She looked even prettier up close.

"You made it!" Laura gave him a big hug. Kevin caught a quick whiff of fruity perfume as her hair brushed his cheeks. "I'm so glad you're here. Are you having a good time? Did you bring your friends?"

"Yeah, they're somewhere around," Kevin said, taking a quick gander around the yard. All of the trash from the party decorated it to create the perfect appearance of wild fun.

"Great! The more the merrier," Laura replied.

"I like your shirt," Kevin said. He did his best to not let his voice crack.

"Oh yeah. Don't you love it?" Laura asked. "I wore it especially for you. You know? Since we both love astrology so much!"

"Definitely." Kevin smiled. His blue eyes sparkled and caught her bright red lips as she smiled and laughed and twirled around in the moonlight.

"Do you dance?" Laura said, grabbing Kevin's hand.

Kevin had never been a believer in fate as much as he was now. Fate, in its generosity, had somehow prompted the band to slow down their music just when he reached the outdoor area, and it was perfect for intimate dancing. Kevin pulled Laura in and held her close as he swayed her back and forth. Nothing else seemed to matter.

☯

Claire wanted to enjoy herself despite this not being her most ideal atmosphere. She was a pure adventurer, and preferred things like camping or chasing down the latest indie band to going to parties. But what she loved most was doing those things with Kevin. For now, she decided to settle on watching Sam try to impress people by balancing plastic red cups on his forehead. She laughed and shook her head in amusement.

"You are just so hot," a shirtless stranger said to Claire. His build gave the impression he was an athlete. "You go to Cambridge?"

"Excuse me?" Claire said.

"Tank. My friends call me Tank." He slurred his words back to her. It was clear he was inebriated.

"Yeah. That still doesn't explain why you're directly in front of my face right now," Claire said, leaning backward.

"Because you're so hot. Girls at Cambridge usually aren't so hot," said Tank.

Claire wanted to punch the guy but figured that would be pointless, given the fact that he didn't look like someone who possessed the sensitivity to feel much of anything.

"You must be the class funny guy," Claire said. "The all-American bully who stuffs smart kids in their lockers. The guy who has a cheerleader for a girl, yet showers with the jocks. I get it. You say a few words and most girls probably think you're cute—like a puppy. The problem is, I don't find your act cute."

"My act?" Tank asked confused.

"Just please leave," Claire demanded, pushing him as far away from her as her arms could reach.

She folded her arms and looked the other way. A few people who had noticed the interaction snickered, enjoying the spectacle of the arrogant Tank humbled and sent looking for another prospect. Claire took a deep breath. Although she was flattered, she had standards … and bigger fish to fry. Her mind wandered back to the earlier message from Z. She hoped Kevin was okay.

"Wow. I thought that was so cool what you just did," said Gracie. "To see you turn down that hot guy. Wow."

"Uhh, thanks," said Claire, confused.

"My name's Gracie." A wide grin was plastered across her face.

"Hi, Gracie. Claire."

"I know. You're friends with Kevin right?" Gracie asked.

"Yeah actually. But how did you—" Claire asked.

"Oh. Don't freak out. I'm a friend of Laura's," Gracie explained.

"Got it," Claire said. Claire marshaled her inner detective skills and decided to keep an eye on Gracie. After what happened at the library, she was convinced that anybody could be "Z." She knew *somebody* was watching them.

"I hear the band outside is really cool," Gracie said. "I knew the lead singer once. Well, I know who he dated. Long story. Would love to share sometime. Anyways ... want to check it out and reject some more hot guys?"

If Claire hadn't pegged her as a cyber criminal, she might have laughed and agreed. Instead, she proceeded with caution.

"Sure," Claire said. "Why not?"

☙

"Want to see me balance ten red cups now?" Sam asked.

He put his head down as his fifth attempt to make friends was met with demeaning snickers and rude remarks. He'd hoped to at least make Claire laugh, but felt discouraged after she walked past him to go outside with a random girl. Regardless, he knew he needed to focus on his task at hand. Sam's plan now was to avoid looking like he was scouting the party. If someone like Z was spying on him and his friends, he had to be sure to have the upper hand. He gave the party another glance. Claire was nowhere in sight anymore. He figured it would be best to head outside, and looked at his phone to make note of the time.

"New text message," Sam mumbled to himself. "I don't recognize this number though."

Sam opened the text and his stomach dropped. It was Z.

> *From 617-682-7897 at 10:34pm: I told you to watch your back. Hope you enjoy the rest of the party.—Z*

Sam looked around once more. This made the message all the more of a mystery. He thought for a moment and then realized that this was his first clue. It was evident that Z did not want to be seen—that's why he or she didn't want to use their real name. Sam concluded that this meant Z had to be someone they knew. He decided to text back to see if anyone nearby would pick up their phone.

> *From Sam at 10:35pm: Gotcha!*

He looked around to see if anyone was texting. Everyone was. And although there was no clue of the culprit, there was an instant response.

> *From 617-682-7897 at 10:35pm: Nice try ;)—Z*

Sam hurried outside to find his friends. He had to tell them. He couldn't keep them in the dark about all this astrological madness any longer.

✦

Kevin cheered with Laura and the crowd after the band finished their intimate set. He looked at her, and she bared a genuine grin. Everything was going exactly how he imagined it would. It was as if everything he had gone through with Susan was finally behind him. He was beginning to fall for Laura.

"Do you want something to drink?" Laura asked. "Kevin?"

Kevin was embarrassed—he had almost forgotten where he was. He snapped out of his trance. "Sorry," he said, shaking his head.

"It's okay," Laura said, and she flashed a smile at him. "I just asked if you might want a drink or something."

"Uhh, sure. That sounds good," Kevin said.

"Great. I'll be right back." She winked at him.

Kevin watched Laura head off to the patio bar and began to fix his shirt, unbuttoning one more button and giving himself a pep talk. *This is it*, he thought to himself. He was ready to ask her out on a date.

"Thank god I found you," Sam said, as he wiped the sweat dripping off his forehead. "Where's Laura?"

"Just left," Kevin said. "Are you okay? You're sweating like crazy right now."

"Actually, no," Sam said. "Well ... it's a long story and I don't want you to get the wrong idea or think I'm insane, but—"

"You two look like you're having fun," said Claire. She walked up with Gracie, who was just as eager to hang out with everyone.

"Hi, Kevin. Hi, Sam" said Gracie. Her tumultuous energy made her look like she was shaking.

Sam was confused and unexcited when he looked at her. "Umm, who are you?" he asked.

"I'm Gracie."

"I'm sure you are," Sam said. "Right now isn't a good time. Please excuse us."

"Don't be rude, Sam," Claire said. "Geez. We just came over to say hi."

"I know, man. What's your deal?" Kevin asked.

"What's my deal?" Sam asked, now getting annoyed. "What's my deal is that we're being spied on by some sort of cyber terrorist and no one is giving me the time of day so that I can actually warn you guys."

"Whoa. Wait, what?" Kevin said, holding his hand up. "Slow down. I'm not sure I'm following. Or are you just joking around?"

"He's not," said Claire, and everybody fell silent, now ready to listen. "Whoever it is knows about our Zodiac journey. And the mistresses. And … and probably Laura."

"Wait, you knew about this?" Sam asked, looking at Claire. "Since when?"

"Yeah," Claire said. "I was sent a creepy anonymous message while I was on the library computer today."

"Great. Just great," Kevin said. "I finally meet a new and amazing girl, and you guys, my best friends, are keeping important information from me? Information that could potentially mess my chances up?"

"What's going on?" Laura said, as she walked up with drinks in her hands. She paused and gave Gracie a cold stare. "What … the … *hell* are you doing here?"

Gracie looked more nervous than usual. "Umm … Hi, Laura. Great party," she said.

"You … YOU are not supposed to be here!" Laura shrieked as she threw the drinks down to the ground.

Kevin, Claire, and Sam froze, totally confused. Neither of them knew what was going on. They looked at each other in dismay as Laura lunged for Gracie's throat.

"Get out!" Laura screamed.

Laura pushed Gracie to the ground. At that moment, the crowd grew silent as their attention was captured by the two warriors brawling on the grass. Kevin did his best to grab Laura, who was winning by a long shot. Claire chipped in by helping to rescue Gracie. Sam, whose idea of heroism was a bit more subtle than most, took out his camera phone and began recording.

"Sam!" Claire yelled. "Seriously? Would you help us already?"

"Sorry," Sam said. Embarrassed, he placed his phone back in his pocket.

The crowd made taunting remarks as the two fighters were broken up. Thankfully, the damage amounted to only a few tears in Gracie's clothes, and some small cuts and bumps, which would likely turn into bruises over time. Laura did her best to kick away from Kevin for another attempt at combat—her eyes had an angry glow in them. Gracie's tears motivated Kevin to hold onto Laura tighter; he knew that Gracie could suffer much worse damage if he let go.

"Let go of me!" Laura yelled at Kevin.

Gracie had gotten back up and was brushing dirt and grass off her clothes. She wiped a stream of tears from her face, looked back at the three friends, mumbled a few words that sounded like "I'm sorry, I'm just sorry," and dashed off. Kevin let go of Laura once Gracie was out of sight, and Laura stormed off inside.

"You guys better clear out quick," said a random student. "I heard the neighbors just called the cops—Laura's parents won't be happy if they find out we were all here."

Sam looked at Claire and nodded.

"Hey guys, I'm gonna stay here," Kevin said as he looked back at Laura. "Laura is pretty shaken up. I'll catch up with you guys tomorrow?"

"Sure," Sam said.

Kevin looked at Claire for approval.

"Yeah. Go. We get it. We'll see you tomorrow," Claire said. Her heart stung.

Claire and Sam looked at each other with identical concern. They knew losing their friend this evening was inevitable.

Laura winced. "Ouch," she said scrunching her nose in pain.

"Sorry," Kevin said as he added more rubbing alcohol to a wet cloth. "It's probably going to sting just a bit more."

Kevin applied the towel to Laura's cheek and took a look around him. Laura's bathroom mirrored the magnificence of the rest of her home. Now that everything had settled down and the cops had kicked everyone out, his focus on all of the little things became clear. Kevin had almost forgotten entirely about what had just happened; he was absorbed with Laura's charm as she leaned over the sink, hoping there would be no permanent marks left from her fight with Gracie. He didn't know what to make of the evening. It was all a bit much. One thing he did know was that he had feelings for Laura, and they were strong enough to allow him to overlook Laura's recent outbursts.

"Thanks," Laura said.

"You don't have to—" Kevin said.

"No really. I do," Laura said. "You've been so sweet through all of this. I feel like such a mess."

"You're not a mess," Kevin said. He handed her another wet towel.

"I don't know what happened," Laura said, shaking her head. It was as if she was waking up from a coma. "I just saw Gracie and a bunch of stuff from our past came up. We used to be best friends but recently had a falling out. I lost control. I'm sorry you had to see that. That's not me, really."

Kevin appreciated her apology. He needed the reassurance that she was more than the Aries described in Kubo's book. He wanted to hope that this would be the only thing he needed to pursue.

"Your friends probably think I'm some sort of crazy person," Laura said.

"What, them?" Kevin said. "No. Not at all. They like you. They told me themselves. This was totally not a big deal."

Both of them knew that wasn't the case, but Laura appreciated the kind words.

Kevin looked down at his watch. "Hey, it's getting late. I should probably get going."

Laura gave a half smile. "Okay. I'll walk you to the door."

As they walked through the living room past the mounds of empty red plastic cups on the floor and half-eaten pizzas, Kevin tried to gather up the courage he'd had after the band had played their last song before the fight. He decided the goodbye would be the perfect moment. He just had to recite it in his head to ensure the right tone.

Laura, I like you. Do you want to … No, no, no. That's not it. Laura, I think you're really awesome. No. No. That's not it either.

His time was up. The door was now the only thing that stood between him and his ambition.

"Well, despite all the drama, I had a good time with you tonight, mister," Laura said giving Kevin a playful poke to the chest. She kept her hand there, resting it near Kevin's heart.

"Yeah, it was great," Kevin said, feeling butterflies in his stomach at her touch. "And all things considered, I think you have some pretty awesome martial arts skills."

Laura laughed, and the pause that followed made her anticipation all the more obvious.

"Hey, so ... do you want to go out sometime? Like on a date?" Kevin asked.

"After everything tonight?" Laura asked. "Really? You're not running for the hills?"

"Nope. Well, actually, I'm not much of a runner," Kevin said.

Laura laughed again and then sighed. "You're something else, Kevin Deer. And yes, I'd love to."

She grabbed him by the collar and kissed him. It was everything Kevin could have dreamt of and more. He kissed her back and brushed one hand through her hair, and pulling her in closer to him with his other hand. For a moment, it felt as if it were just the two of them in the world. When they stopped, Kevin swore he saw little stars sparkling in her green eyes, as if they were lining up for him.

"Goodnight," Laura said, looking down at her toes with a shy smile.

Kevin walked back to his dorm with a new beat in his step. The night had been life-changing. As he looked back in the direction of Laura's house, he made an effort to reflect and savor everything that had just happened. He had no idea where this journey would take him, but he was loving every moment of it so far.

☺

The next day at the dorms, Claire and Sam waited for Kevin. They had planned to meet up and discuss their cyber-stalker. It was time to put everything out on the table and figure out if there was some kind of connection they should be seeing. Kubo's death, Laura's behavior, and the most important matter—figuring out who "Z" was. Claire and Sam were getting worked up as they exchanged their own secrets about Z. And while the mystery was a bit creepy, it made for exciting dialogue.

"This is crazy," Claire said. "So you haven't given your number out since Senior Recruitment Day, and you're getting texts from this weirdo?"

"You are correct," Sam said as he munched his favorite snack—freshly popped popcorn.

"I don't get it though. Why does Z even care about us doing this Zodiac journey?" Claire asked.

"I don't know. I thought about that too." Sam replied. He ripped a page out of his English notebook and grabbed a Sharpie marker off his desk. "Okay, so our first encounter with Z was the day we found out Kubo died, right?" He wrote at the top of the page, "Z—Potential Suspects" and drew a line under it. Then he wrote KUBO underneath it and drew a big X through Kubo's name.

"I'm not following you. What's your point?" Claire said.

"That is my point," Sam said, tapping Kubo's crossed out name. "Process of elimination. Kubo couldn't be Z since he's dead."

"Way to honor his death, Sherlock," Claire said shaking her head.

"Yeah? Well, go on. Do you have any better ideas?" Sam said as he tossed the marker at her.

Claire grabbed the marker, which hadn't even come close to hitting her, and tore out a second page from Sam's notebook. She began to draw a diagram similar to a spider web on the page.

"Relax," Claire said. "It's not the worst idea you've ever had. Okay, so let's think."

She proceeded to write names on the meeting points of the web. Sam looked on at her handiwork and decided to just stick to his popcorn.

"Okay now," Claire said pulling her hair up in a messy bun. "Professor Kubo, Professor Thompson, Laura, Gracie, and random library guy. These are our suspects so far. Professor Kubo died, so I agree with you—we can cross his name off the list of suspects." Claire drew an X through Kubo's name on her diagram. "But Laura was the one who introduced Kevin to Kubo's class in the first place. That was our first encounter with her right?"

"Yep. I definitely remember that," Sam said. "And I remember the way she tackled Gracie. Sheesh. She's probably like a Russian spy or something."

Claire rolled her eyes. "Stay with me here. Kubo mysteriously died after Kevin accidentally got a hold of his book. Other than the articles I showed you earlier, we don't know too much else about Kubo."

"What about Gracie?" Sam asked.

"Ehh. I don't know," Claire said. "I was with Gracie while we were at the party and I didn't see her use her phone at all. You said Z was texting you during the party right?"

"Yeah," Sam said. "But there's all kinds of software for that these days. She could have even had someone else do it for her."

"Okay. We'll keep her on here for now," Claire said. "So. What do you think? Kubo's dead. Gracie was with me. Laura …"

Both Claire and Sam paused as fright gripped their reality.

"We have to warn Kevin," Claire said, circling Laura's name and writing the words, "Z?" next to it.

☙

Laura bit her bottom lip and played with the dainty gold "L" shaped charm on her necklace as the waiter approached to take her and Kevin's order. She had straightened her curly hair and smoothed it back into an elegant updo that made her look like a model for a bridal magazine. She was wearing a beautiful, short, black cocktail dress that was covered in rhinestones at the bottom. Her shoulders were exposed and it looked like she had dusted some glitter along her collarbone. Kevin, who had never been to a restaurant this fancy before, was excited to experience the prestige with her. He had on his best suit jacket—a beautiful black with satin lapels—which he typically reserved for school dances or funerals.

The energy shined like gold. Each napkin was folded carefully to look like a flower in bloom, and there were notes of beautiful classical music playing in the background. Yet, even with all of these fine elements, the one thing that stood out most was sitting across from him.

"So what do you think of this place?" Laura asked.

"It's great," Kevin replied, trying to remember what silverware was used for what.

Laura let out a deep breath of satisfaction and relief. "This place is one of my favorites. I know it's very fancy, but I really wanted to share this with you. I'm glad you like it," she said.

As much as Kevin wanted to return the sentiment, he found himself struggling to pay attention. His phone was going off for the fifth time now, and the constant vibration was distracting him. And although he did his best to play it off, Laura noticed and frowned at him.

"Is there something wrong?" She asked.

"Nope. No, nothing wrong," Kevin said as he scratched the back of his head. "Umm, do you mind if I excuse myself, just for a second?"

"Sure," Laura said with a sigh as she adjusted herself in her chair. She was clearly annoyed but trying to stay calm.

Kevin got up from the table and walked to the lobby of the restaurant to check the commotion coming from his phone.

"Fourteen missed calls," he read. Five missed calls were from Claire and the other nine were from Sam. He dialed back the most recent number and looked over to see how Laura was doing. Her body language spelled aggravated.

"Hello. Dude! You're alive. Oh, thank goodness," Sam said.

"What the heck is going on you guys?" Kevin said, doing his best to whisper. "I'm kind of in the middle of a date with Laura here."

"Yeah. That may be a problem," Sam said.

"What are you talking about?" Kevin asked. He looked around embarrassed when he realized he might have spoken louder than he'd meant to. He lowered his voice on the second attempt. "What are you talking about?"

"Kevin, we think Laura could be the cyberstalker we started to tell you about the other night at her party," Claire said, chiming in.

"You guys can't be serious," Kevin replied. "I'm on a date. With *her*. Like right now. What do you expect me to do?"

Sam hopped back on the phone. "You should break things off. Tell her you're sick or make something else up," he said.

"I'm not going to do that. Listen, I like Laura, okay? I was hoping that my *best* friends would support me on this. I gotta go."

"Kevin, wait—" Sam said.

Kevin hung up before he could hear more of Sam's plea and took another glance around. He decided to ignore the cold stares and head back to his table. Laura was visibly upset and stared at Kevin—it was clear she wanted an explanation of some kind.

"Sorry," Kevin said. "Family emergency."

"So are you going to tell me what's really going on?" Laura said.

"Huh? I don't know what you mean …" Kevin replied.

Laura huffed and crossed her arms in front of her. "All the calls, the texts. Whatever it is. You're being so distant, Kevin. On our first real date? After our … moment the other night, I thought you really liked me."

"I do like you. I do," Kevin said, as he reached across the table to grab one of her hands and gave it a reassuring squeeze. "That wasn't about anything. Really. You've got to trust me."

They were interrupted by their waiter. "Here are your appetizers," he said, as he placed two plates down in front of each of them. "The fried calamari for you, sir, and the butternut crostini for you, miss."

"Thank you," Kevin said, as he laid his napkin on his lap.

Kevin looked back at Laura, who stared at her plate with her fists balled up.

"Is everything okay, miss?" the waiter asked.

"Uhh, no. Clearly not! What do you think I just ordered? Tell me!" She yelled.

The waiter began to tremble. "I'm sorry, miss. But you did order this," he said.

"No. It's all wrong!" Laura screamed. "I did not order a crostini. Take it back!" She pushed her plate away from her and threw her napkin on the table.

"Miss, this *is* what you ordered. I assure you," said the waiter, confused.

Kevin understood the waiter's confusion. The order wasn't messed up. It *was* what Laura had ordered. Kevin looked at her to try to understand why she was being so erratic.

"Take ... It ... Back!" Laura yelled.

Kevin pushed himself backward in his chair as she proceeded to swipe the dishes off of the table and onto the floor. The waiter was covered in bits of butternut squash and tartar sauce. Laura, who showed no remorse, huffed and puffed from across the table.

"Is there a problem here?" another waiter hurriedly approached their table. He had a more senior air about him than the waiter covered in scraps. Kevin assumed he was a manager or supervisor.

"Yes!" Laura shouted as she pointed at the other waiter. "Your idiot excuse for a waiter over here messed up our order and ruined our first date!"

Kevin looked at the manager with a nervous sweat. He could feel the stares from other tables. He looked at Laura, who was not calming down, and he was glad there was no more food on the table. Kevin tried to speak but he didn't know how to respond.

"Miss, I'm sorry, but we are going to have to ask you to leave," said the manager in a quiet but stern voice.

"Why should I leave? We are paying customers," Laura demanded. "*He's* the one who messed up our order." She stomped one foot on the floor and pointed at the original waiter.

"Miss, we are asking you very nicely. If you don't want to cooperate, we will have to call the police," the manager said as he gestured to the front door.

"Whoa, hold on, there's no need for that," Kevin said. "It's all right, we'll leave."

As Kevin put his arm around Laura's waist and they walked to the door, he noticed the looks on everyone's faces. It was demeaning, but he knew he couldn't abandon Laura right now. She was his Aries. She was his only shot now at true love. Kevin hailed for a cab and put his suit jacket over Laura's shoulders.

"Thanks, Kevin," she said sheepishly. She picked at one of the rhinestones of her dress and Kevin could tell she was embarrassed. He and opened the taxi door for her.

"So I'll call you later?" Kevin asked. He leaned in and gave Laura a kiss goodbye.

Laura nodded—she recognized that the damage had been done. It was a silent and apologetic gesture. Kevin understood its sincerity. As the cab drove off, he pulled out his phone to text her. He wanted to tell her how none of her outbursts mattered to him. He wanted to tell her he cared. Instead, he was met with an alarming surprise. It was a text message he had received while Laura was arguing with the waiters. It was from a number he didn't recognize.

> *From 617-682-7897 at 8:18pm: And the walls will come tumbling down soon enough. —Z*

It was enough of a distraction to make him forget about Laura. *Sam and Claire were right*, he thought to himself. He decided to go straight to Sam's dorm and hoped both of his friends would still be there.

❧

"Okay. I'm ready to listen. Explain everything," Kevin said.

Claire and Sam hovered over their hand-drawn chart of suspects and took turns sharing their individual encounters with Z. It was a whirlwind of information. All of it made sense just as much as none of it made sense. There was no straight answer for any of it, but it was clear that there was a bigger picture to all of this.

"Guys, it just can't be Laura," Kevin said.

"Why not?" Sam asked.

"Because … well … because I got a text from Z too, when I was at the restaurant with Laura. And it couldn't be Laura because she was fighting with the waiters when I got the text."

"Wait … Z texted you too?" Sam asked.

"A fight? What happened?" Claire asked, more concerned with finding out how the date had gone than about Z.

Kevin pulled out his phone and showed them the text. Sam grabbed his phone to study the message and compare it to the one he had on his own phone. Kevin continued, "It wasn't a fist fight like with Gracie or anything. She may have just—"

"Just what?" Claire asked. She threw her hands in the air, waiting for an answer.

"She may have just thrown our food at one of the waiters," Kevin said. He couldn't meet Claire's eyeline—he knew that she would make him feel terrible.

"Kevin. This is serious," Claire said. "She has an anger problem. You can't see that? First her fight with Gracie, and now this?"

"Oh, and don't forget what happened in class," Sam said.

Kevin frowned and signaled him to keep quiet.

"What? What happened in class?" Claire asked.

"Oops." Sam knew he had blurted out too much.

"Spill it," Claire said.

"Okay, fine," Kevin said as he gave Sam another frown. "Laura may have had an angry outburst in class right before her party."

"Geez, Kevin," Claire said.

Kevin put his head down. "Okay, you're right. This is messed up. I just … I like her a lot. I was finally starting to get over Susan," he said with a sigh.

"You're going to have to end it you know?" Claire said. She was trying her best to hide her excitement.

"Maybe this is what Z meant by that text. The walls tumbling down," Kevin said. "All right, I'll end it with Laura. I think she probably knows it's coming—after her outburst at the restaurant, she must know. But I'm not giving up on true love. I'm sticking with this guys. I can't lose my chance."

Claire and Sam looked at each other; they understood. Their friend needed this. If the legend from Kubo's book was true, losing out on love wouldn't be worth giving up after one bad date. Sam handed Kevin back his phone. Kevin looked at the device as if it were some sort of punishment. He clicked on Laura's number. It was time.

☽

A week had gone by since Kevin had sent Laura his final text, and he hadn't heard from her or seen any sign of her. He sat back in his chair as the class ended. Astrology just wasn't the same anymore. He looked at Sam who knew how he was feeling.

"So that concludes our lecture for today," Thompson said as the students began to pack their bags to leave. "I've posted everyone's current grades online, so be sure to look at them and ask me any questions you may have. For your midterm, we are going to make it an interactive exam this year—more on that later. And don't forget that tonight I will be at the observatory, where you can get some extra credit, if you need it."

"So what do you think?" Sam said.

"About what?" Kevin asked dazed.

"About tonight," Sam said. He wanted to cheer his friend up. "Should we go to the observatory? I know we're both passing the class, but it could be fun."

"Sure," Kevin replied. His enthusiasm was absent.

Sam could feel the apathy in Kevin's demeanor. "Look man, I get it," he said, "but there's still a week and a half left of the Aries cycle. This doesn't mean you have to give up. You can still find love. Maybe we'll meet an Aries tonight at the observatory." He patted Kevin's back.

"She was just so perfect," Kevin said, looking at Laura's empty desk.

"Yeah, perfectly angry ... and lethal," Sam muttered. "C'mon, forget about her, man. Let's invite Claire to come tonight with us. I'm sure she will help us find another Aries."

Kevin's acceptance of the invitation was interrupted by Professor Thompson clearing his throat just a couple of feet away from his desk.

"Mr. Deer?" Thompson asked. "May I have a moment please?"

Kevin looked at Sam, who shrugged his shoulders. They both had a small fear that they had done something wrong, and braced themselves for the worst.

"You don't need to worry," Thompson said. "Your grades are fine. This is concerning your friend Miss Laura. She's been gone for a week now. I know you two were ... fond of each other."

"Yeah well, actually ... we recently broke up," Kevin said.

"Ah. I see. How unfortunate," Thompson paused for a moment. "Well, if you do see her, please alert her that she is failing my course."

Kevin nodded with a sinking feeling in his gut.

"That will be all," Thompson said. He turned and walked back to the blackboard and started to wipe it clean of the astrology sketches from the class.

As difficult as it was, Kevin decided to let it go. All that mattered now was tonight's assignment. He and Sam met Claire out in the hall and shared their new plan to find another Aries.

☾

"This was so worth it," Sam said. He let out a breath of fresh night air and loosened his uniform tie a bit.

The observatory was marvelous, as usual. Almost every student from Professor Thompson's class was gathered on the top of the tower to collect their extra credit. They were also awarded with a view of perfectly cloudless skies. The stars seemed to dance at the attention.

"I'll admit that it is pretty cool. Thanks for letting me tag along for this," Claire said.

"Of course. Are you kidding? We couldn't come here without you," Sam replied. "By the way, if anyone asks, you're in the earlier class making up for an assignment."

"Sure, you got it Boss," Claire said with a laugh and play-fully hit Sam's arm. Sam was glad it was so dark so that Claire couldn't make out how happy he was to have her attention.

"Yeah, but where's Thompson?" asked Kevin, looking at his phone. "He's like a half hour late."

"Maybe he's in his office passing out F's to everyone," Sam said.

"Come on," Kevin said. "That's not funny, man. Laura is already going through enough as it is. She was crazy upset when I told her she—"

"Wait, *you* told her she was failing?" Sam asked. His eyes widened as he sat back up and gave Kevin a look.

"Yeah. Like that was smart," Claire muttered and rolled her eyes. "Telling someone with an anger problem that she's failing a class. On top of that, the message came from the boy who broke up with her. Great idea, Kev."

"Yeah, maybe I didn't think that one all the way through," Kevin said. He wished he could take the text back.

"Wait. Do you hear something?" Sam said as he ran to look over the railing of the observatory. "What the—"

They heard somebody screaming, "Help! Help! Help!"

Everyone rushed to the railing to see the commotion down below. It was Professor Thompson running for dear life, with his hands flailing over his head.

Behind him in hot pursuit was a campus golf cart going at full speed. Kevin looked at Claire and Sam in a cold sweat as he recognized Laura as the driver.

"This can't be happening," Kevin said. He rushed down the stairs to help. His friends followed quickly behind him.

Laura had cornered the worn-down professor. Thompson crouched down low and panted for air as he reached his hand out to plead without speaking.

"First, you fail me in your class! Then you have the nerve to deliver the message through my ex-boyfriend! You are scum! Absolute scum!" Laura screamed from the driver's seat.

The engine revved up. Thompson lacked the strength to stand, much less apologize. Laura knew this and decided to move forward with her meltdown.

"Laura?" Kevin shouted from the entryway of the observatory. "What are you doing?"

"Kevin?" Laura asked and looked toward the doorway. "I'm … I'm so sorry. He's just … I'm just giving him what he deserves. I'm sorry you have to see this."

"No, this isn't you Laura," Kevin said as he walked over to Thompson as cautiously as he could.

"Kevin, be careful," Claire shouted from behind him.

Laura looked up to see everyone on the balcony watching them intently. She began to cry tears of frustration and anger. As they trickled down her face, she became more enraged. She focused her gaze back on Professor Thompson. Kevin recognized the look in her eye as the same look she'd given to the waiter before she threw her dinner at him, the same look she'd given to Gracie before she pounced on her, and the same look from her first outburst in Thompson's class. Before he could say anything else, Laura slammed her foot on the gas and lost control.

Clouds of smoke and debris launched everywhere. It was like a nuclear explosion had gone off. As the smoke settled, so did the commotion. Kevin had acted quickly enough to pull Thompson away right before he would have been hit, causing Laura to slam the golf cart straight into one of the columns of the observatory wall. Other than a bruised ego and a heavy limp, the professor was shaken up but fine. Everyone's attention now turned to Laura. Despite the totaled golf cart, a bloody nose, and a failed plan, she appeared to be fine as well. She looked at Kevin, and tears welled up in her eyes as she saw the campus police driving up to the observatory.

"I'm so sorry, Kevin," Laura cried. "I'm so sorry."

Kevin, Claire, and Sam stared at the letter on the table for what seemed to be an eternity. It had been a week since Laura's arrest and expulsion, and this was her first attempt to contact Kevin since it was reported that her parents had sent her off to a wellness facility meant to help her get a handle on her anger issues.

"So this is how it ends, huh?" Kevin said with a sigh of defeat. "The search for true love. Done. Over."

Claire put her hand on Kevin's shoulder. "Hey. It's not over. It just means we have to figure out another way."

"What about this Z person?" Kevin asked.

"I don't know," Claire said. "None of us have heard from him or her, right? I guess they decided to call quits. Maybe this got too intense for them, too."

"So are you going to open it?" Sam asked, changing the subject. He was very interested in finding out what the letter said.

"It's just crazy how this all happened," Claire said. "Now she's stuck at a treatment center. No friends. No phones or computers. Nothing. I almost kinda feel bad for her."

"Yeah, me too," Sam said, and repeated, "Okay so … are we going to open the letter now?"

Claire rolled her eyes. "Geez, Sam. Cool your jets."

Kevin picked the letter up and took his time opening it. He felt a connection to it. Perhaps it would give him the closure he needed. He read it without saying a word and was nourished by each sentence. The apologies, the references, the memories; they all made for the perfect sonnet. And as he finished the end of the letter, he couldn't help but smile.

"What's that smile for?" Sam asked. "What did she say?"

Sam took the letter from Kevin and proceeded to read it. Claire sat next to Sam and read it with him. Once they finished they looked up at Kevin, who looked alive and happy. His face was full of color and his eyes sparkled with glee again. Regardless of everything that happened, regardless of the craziness, the letter contained the three words that mattered most.

"*I love you,*" Laura wrote.

It was the perfect ending to a letter and the perfect beginning to the next phase.

"We have to keep going," Sam said, folding the letter up and putting it back down on the table. "We have to keep going," he repeated as he looked at Kevin.

Everyone at the table agreed.

CHAPTER III

—THE TAURUS WHO TALKED TOO MUCH—

Taurus: April 20th—May 21st

The Taurus, a dependable earth sign, is often seen as persistent and loyal but can weave a web of deceit and greed. The Taurus will go out of their way to treat all those around them as incredibly special, but this same attitude can lend itself to create that of a selfish nature in the Taurus. The Taurus are often so goal-oriented that they form a notion that the world revolves around them. Their self-indulgent streak makes them rude, and ignorant of others' emotions. As they aim for complete honesty in their lives, they often overshare information and will be sure to confront any who disagree with their message. For the Taurus Mistress, perseverance to getting the task at hand done right and done to secure their own future will often lead to rash decisions. For Kevin and his friends, this may test the trust they hold in genuine relationships.

"Okay," Claire said, as she plopped a large, plain paper bag on the table. "New game plan."

Kevin and Sam looked at her, confused. They had hoped Claire had found a better substitute for their usual sandwich spot, which they were growing tired of, but they were mistaken. Claire pulled each sandwich from the bag, one by one. Sam ripped open the one marked "Sam" to find his usual meatball sub—he was happy to know Claire paid attention to the things he liked. Kevin pushed his sandwich aside, as he was more curious to hear about Claire's new plan.

"I've been doing some thinking," Claire said, unwrapping her sandwich—she always went with the plain turkey and cheddar. She took a bite and then looked at Sam and Kevin. "If we're going to do this, we need to do it right. Which means we have to be fully prepared. Well, we have to help Kevin to be fully prepared."

Claire took a large box of latex condoms out of the brown bag, and Sam spit out the meatball he had been munching on, which burst out of his mouth like confetti. Kevin and Sam were both speechless. They had never seen so many condoms before. Sam didn't want to admit it, but he had never actually owned a box of condoms before in his life.

"Claire?" Sam asked. "What the heck are you doing with a forty count box of condoms?"

"That's for me to know, and for you to find out," Claire said grinning.

Neither Kevin or Sam said a word. Claire shook her head at them and rolled her eyes.

"Really? You guys seriously think these are all for me?" Claire said. "They're not for me, geniuses. They're for Kevin. Obviously." She pushed the box toward Kevin.

"*Me?*" Kevin asked as he awkwardly picked the box up.

"Yes, you," Claire said. "Kevin, you're going to be meeting a lot of girls or 'mistresses of the Zodiac,' or whatever you want to call them, to make this happen. And you might have sex with some of them. I'd rather know you're going to be responsible in the event that happens. Does original latex work?"

"Uhh, sure, I guess," Kevin said.

Kevin, although he wasn't, might as well have been a virgin. His first and only experience had been with Susan—a moment he hated re-living. It was a torturous memory that reminded him just how much he missed her. Even so, he trusted Claire's advice and decided she was probably right—he should at least be prepared. He opened the box and took a few out. He felt awkward handling these in front of his two friends, and he noticed Claire looking at him intently. What he didn't see was the jealousy on her face that she tried to hide.

"Okay, next … there's these," Claire said, pulling out three small brown leather booklets.

"What are these?" Sam asked.

Kevin opened one of the books. It was a Zodiac calendar along with a summary of each sign. Each sign was highlighted next to its cycle date and had a detailed synopsis of all its main personality traits. Kevin was fascinated. Every drop of information painted an image of each sign with precision. And yet, each mistress still remained a mystery waiting to be solved.

"These are so we can have a better grasp of each sign," Claire said. "I cross-referenced it with Kubo's book and it's the most accurate summary of each sign based on that."

"Nice," Sam said excited. "We're officially like Eleven and her friends in *Stranger Things*. Except a little older, I guess. And no freaky underworld."

"Who?" Claire asked.

"You know?" Sam said. "Eleven? The Upside Down? Only the greatest new show out right now? Friends, adventure, the supernatural, bad guys. Yeah?"

Kevin and Claire laughed.

"Seriously, Sam," Claire said. "You have got to get out more."

"Yeah, yeah," Sam replied, disappointed. He had hoped Claire would understand his TV show reference and appreciate his pop culture knowledge.

"What's that?" Kevin asked as Claire pulled out a small black smartphone.

"This?" Claire asked holding it up for Kevin and Sam to see. "This is what I'd like to call your 'little black book.'"

"I don't get it," Kevin said. "Why do I need that?"

"Let me explain," Claire said. "So, you technically only have one month to find love with a girl from each phase right? And it has to happen *during* that phase, right?"

"Yeah, you're right," Kevin said, still not understanding where Claire was going with this.

"Right," Claire said. "So that means you need to work fast. So, I just got this basic smartphone from the on-campus tech center. They're cheap knock-off phones, so they're not anything fancy, but you can still download apps on it. I downloaded

'Cupid Academy Connect.' It's a dating app made for boarding school students. Best part is ... a person's birthday and age is the first thing that show up on his or her profile. I took the liberty of creating a profile for you."

"Claire, I *really* don't want to be on a dating app," Kevin insisted. He pushed the phone back towards her. "I already explained to Sam that I believe this should happen organically—through *fate*. Just like it says in Kubo's book. Think about how this whole journey transpired. If the universe wants to put me on this quest, the universe will make it happen."

"Ughhh, Kev," Claire groaned. She was annoyed. "I know you think that but we may not always have time to just 'let things happen.'"

Sam stepped in. "Kevin, I think I actually agree with Claire on this. With 'Z' now involved and everything that happened with Laura, I think it's wise we take as much control as we can." He picked up the thin smartphone and handed it to Kevin. "It's the only way."

Kevin sighed. "Okay, but for the record, I'm not *in love* with the idea."

Kevin clicked open the app and Sam stared in awe. This colorful app had clearly been designed for students who were looking to have fun at their boarding school or with others their age who happened to live nearby but attended another school. As Kevin swiped left and right on each profile to give them a better sense of it, the plan became more clear. This would be a much quicker and easier way for Kevin to meet the specific Zodiac sign he needed to encounter without having to waste time searching everywhere for that person. Every digital icon, upbeat clicking noise, and flirtatious picture displayed heightened their excitement about this adventure. Kevin eased up on the idea as he felt he was getting closer to true love, Claire felt closer to Kevin, and Sam felt closer to Claire. They each had their motives, and they all wanted the same thing.

ꙮ

There was something comforting about the smell of pine in the dormitories that next day. Kevin sat in his dorm room reflecting on all the events that had transpired over the last month. He looked over at his dresser and saw the items Claire had given him for his quest. He shook his head. He admired Claire, and he was grateful for all her help. She always was the prepared one.

Despite everything Claire had done, Kevin wasn't exactly feeling excited. He couldn't quite place it, but he was feeling a sense of emptiness. He decided to fill that void by picking up the smartphone Claire had given him. He clicked open his Cupid Academy Connect app and saw his profile picture staring back at him. He hit the plus sign by his photo to add some more pictures. He tapped the camera and flipped it to take a selfie—he flashed a wide grin and snapped the picture, making sure the crisp white collar of his uniform shirt could be seen. He thought that made him look put together.

He then began to scroll through some of the messages he had received since Claire created his account. To his surprise, every girl was unique. Some were dressed in the latest in fashion, while others compensated with plump lips that they formed into a seducing pout in their selfies. It was enough to intrigue him, and one by one, Kevin swiped on any potential match that caught his eye. It was addicting, and after a few moments, he had figured out that he could just keep swiping to select as many as possible. It was a temporary high, but it certainly helped him forget about the feeling of loneliness. He hoped that he would get a match soon.

And he did. A clever little bell sound notified Kevin of his first match on Cupid Academy Connect. But her birthdate was not a Taurus date, so he had to ignore her for now.

"Bummer," Kevin muttered.

He continued sifting through the pool of temptation. This session went on for what many would deem far too long, but Kevin kept it up. After a while, his phone froze and began to scroll on its own. Kevin frantically clicked every button in an attempt to stop it but it was like it had a mind of its own. His phone swiped, scrolled, and liked random photo after photo.

"AUGH!" Kevin slammed it down on his desk.

The screen of his phone started to flash. He picked it up and saw it had finally stopped. He looked at the profile and saw he was in luck. The profile his phone matched was a Taurus. This particular Taurus, however, wasn't just any Taurus. He recognized this person. As he looked closer, he saw that it was Gracie, the girl Laura had gotten into a fight with at her birthday party. But before Kevin could marvel at the coincidence, he got a buzz on his other phone. He recognized the number and opened it with caution as if it were a ticking time bomb.

> From 617-682-7897 at 2:43pm: I see someone still hasn't learned their lesson. Your selfish quest will soon end. —Z

Kevin stared at the message. He thought he had heard the last of Z, and he wanted this to end. He immediately sent a group text to Claire and Sam.

To Claire & Sam at 2:45pm: "Just got a message from Z. We should keep our heads up."

Kevin's concern was interrupted by another phone notification. This time it was on the burner phone. It was a message from Gracie—his first official message on Cupid Academy Connect.

> Hi, Kevin! Fancy meeting you on here :-) I guess this means we're a match? Or did you click me by mistake? Hopefully not. I totally understand if it was though. Was it? Maybe we should meet up. I love cafés, don't you? They remind me of France. I've never been to France though. Have you? Silly question. Of course you have. You seem like a well-traveled man. Anywho ... I know a great place not too far from Cambridge. I've heard that the owner is a bit weird, but that the coffee is great. Lol. What do you say? XO, Gracie

The quirky message was almost enough to make Kevin forget about the message from Z. He thought for a second. Gracie seemed nice. In fact, his memory of her from Laura's party was a positive one. He thought about it again and realized that other than the quick "hello" and then the fight, he didn't really have much of a memory of her at all—Laura had had all of his attention. He did remember that she seemed to run on endless energy. Kevin wondered if maybe he should have paid more attention to Gracie to begin with. He sent a reply.

"Hey, Gracie. Super random right? I'm definitely up for a nice café. Let's do it."

☙

Of the many students who took a seat that day, Sam and Claire were perhaps the most eager. The Journalism Student Union had just begun its open forum club, and both of them thought this would prove useful. Claire, after recent events, felt a spark of passion for the field of investigative journalism. She hoped to find more answers on the matter of Professor Kubo's Zodiac findings, and perhaps even find out a bit more about herself. She figured this would also be the best thing to keep her mind busy, despite her worries about Kevin and his involvement with his potential mistresses.

While Claire's intentions were on the noble side, Sam's interest in the club was a lot simpler: he figured this was a good excuse to be next to Claire. His strategy was to do well in the club and hope it would impress her. His assumption that this plan was foolproof however, would soon prove false.

"Claire? Sam?" asked Gracie. "I had no idea you guys were into journalism. How cool. Hugs."

Gracie reached out to Sam and Claire and gave them each a tight squeeze. Sam pulled away, annoyed and confused.

"Hey, Gracie," Claire responded. "Yeah, I figured this would be a cool club to join. I hear it's a great start if you want to major in the field."

"Of course it's cool," Gracie said. "The JSU is only the *coolest* club Cambridge has ever had. I also just so happen to be the president. You'll fit right in. Most of the time we play news reports on the projector and discuss them after. Have you been keeping up with the latest on the teacher love scandal? Who am I kidding? Of course you have. Drama, drama, drama. Oh and don't get me started on the perks for being in the club. Did I mention the free snacks? It's so much fun!"

Sam rolled his eyes. He could feel his simple plan crumbling with each word Gracie spoke. He also had a feeling in his gut that something wasn't quite right about her, so he took out his phone to distract himself. He noticed the group text from Kevin about Z then looked at Gracie.

"Oh wow. That's awesome," Claire said. "I should take notes from you. I've always wanted to run a club like this."

"Nothing to it but to do it," Gracie said. "Aw, shucks. I'm glad I met you guys—I really like you both. Hey, so, where's Kevin by the way?"

"Kevin?" Claire asked. "Umm—"

"Well, usually you guys are always together," Gracie interrupted and shrugged her shoulders. "I just figured he'd be here too."

"He has another class in like thirty minutes," Claire said. "This didn't fit in his schedule."

"Aww, darn," Gracie said, as she formed her brightly bubblegum colored pink lips into a pout. "Well, if you talk to him before I do, tell him I'm so excited about our café date! Oh gosh, it's going to be amazing. You know I heard the owner—"

"Wait," Sam interrupted her. "Date?"

"Oh. Well, yeah," Gracie said. "Didn't he tell you? We matched up on Cupid Academy Connect this afternoon. We exchanged a couple of messages, but I think we had such a deep connection. It just, oh gosh. It just felt like it all fell into place perfectly. Like it was meant to be. Maybe he could even be '*The One*.'" She opened her eyes wide with excitement and twirled a piece of her black hair around her fingers.

"Great," Claire mumbled.

"Pardon?" Gracie said.

"Oh ... I said that's great," Claire said. "Really great for you guys."

Now Claire and Sam were both uncomfortable. They looked at each other with an awkward grin and then back at Gracie. Sam felt she was a suspect. Claire felt she was competition. It was a tense moment.

"Oh shucks," Gracie said. "Well, I need to head to the front to get everything started now. We absolutely must catch up soon. Promise, promise, promise. Okay. See you afterward."

Gracie trotted off with a giddy hop, her khaki uniform skirt swaying from side to side as she bounced away. Claire and Sam had no idea why that whirlwind of awkwardness had taken place, but it was disappointing for them both. Sam looked at Claire and thought she had the same hunch as he did.

"Who talks like that?" Sam asked. "Really? '*Oh, shucks*'" he said mockingly to Claire. "Are we on a sitcom from the sixties? And she already thinks Kevin is 'The One'—they haven't even had one date! I'm telling you, Claire, something isn't right about her."

"Come on, Sam," Claire said. "Gracie doesn't seem so bad. She's nice. Weird. But nice."

"Yeah, sure," Sam said. "You got the weird part right. I don't know. I'm starting to feel like she has something to do with the whole Z situation."

"Would you keep it down?" Claire asked. "The last thing we need to do is broadcast this mysterious cybertexter to the entire school. What if Z can hear us?"

"Sorry," Sam said. "It's just … well … did you get Kevin's text?"

"I did," Claire said looking for a couple of seats. "And he's right. We should keep our heads up. But that doesn't mean it's Gracie."

"Okay fine," Sam said. "But just think about it, will you? She just shows up mysteriously, causes a fight with Laura—and we still don't even know why—and now she 'randomly' matched with Kevin on Cupid Academy Connect and is going on a date with him? She's the president of the JSU right? They have all types of connections to the media and technology here on campus. Maybe that's how she …"

Sam paused as he noticed Claire had found one seat between two other students, sat down, and taken out her notebook. He looked around and realized there wasn't another seat near her, and put his head down in defeat. He couldn't understand why Claire wouldn't at least believe him and decided to give up for now until he had more evidence. He noticed a few seats near the back of the room and took a seat by himself as the projector begin to play.

"Hey!" Sam whispered to his neighbors and gave them a quick wave.

On his left, he was ignored by a guy who looked annoyed as he opened up his notebook. To his right, he was greeted by a sweeter presence.

"Hi there," said the girl. She had olive skin with high cheekbones that gave her a modelesque look, and her big round eyes made her look like a cute but concerned puppy.

"I'm Sam," Sam said extending his hand.

"Libby," the sweet girl said, returning the gesture with a nervous squeeze.

Sam couldn't help but notice how timid she was. "So ... yeah ... JSU. Totally sucks, right?"

"Yeah. It's not really my thing. I'm just here to support my roommate. It's her first day as president."

Sam's eyes lit up like the projector. He felt that this was the exact thing he needed to figure out the truth about Gracie. He had found his ticket to get the evidence he needed for Claire to believe him.

☙

Kevin sipped his coffee and listened. Then, as if on repeat, he took another sip and listened some more. It was his first date with Gracie, and she was far from shy when it came to indulging in monologues about gossip and shenanigans. Kevin was more amused than tired. He had never listened to someone go on for as long as she did. In less than an hour, Kevin was already privy to details on the most popular couple on campus, which faculty member the English teacher was suspected of having an affair with, and the latest on cat collections. She was like a gossip column that live-tweeted every detail on anybody or anything.

"Hey, so umm ... want to talk about something else?" Kevin said.

Gracie looked guilty. "Oh shucks," she said. "I'm doing it again, aren't I? I didn't mean to go on so much. I know it's not all about me. I guess I'm just really nervous to be with you. I know this is only like, our first date, but I kinda like you, Kevin."

Gracie extended her hand to hold Kevin's. To him, she seemed so open and honest. He felt that it gave her a sweet innocence. It was just enough to help him feel at ease.

"No. It's fine," Kevin said. "I get it. I was nervous to meet up too. And, it's all interesting stuff. The rumors and everything."

"So ... let's change topics. Tell me about yourself," Gracie said blushing. "I want to know everything about you." She gave his hand a squeeze.

"Everything?" Kevin said. "That may be too long a story for a coffee date."

Gracie laughed. "I know. That was a silly question. How about ... your most embarrassing moment?" she asked.

Kevin froze for a split second. He knew the answer to that question, and he recalled it vividly—Senior Recruitment Day, and his failed profession of love to Susan. No matter how hard he tried to forget it, it was still fresh in his head. Before he could brush the subject off with a white lie, Gracie gave him a smile and squeezed his hand a little tighter. It was enough to make him relax and trust.

"Well," Kevin said, "I pretty much got denied when I tried to give my ex-girlfriend a promise ring and asked her to promise her love to me for forever."

"What? Kind of like a proposal? But you're so young," Gracie said. "Tell me more." Gracie's smile gave Kevin a warm feeling, like he could trust her with anything.

It felt good for him to vent. It was the first time he'd spoken about the incident in this much detail since it had happened. The ring, the jumbotron, the jokes, and the heartbreak all made for a poetic misfortune. He was being more vulnerable than he had been in quite some time. He felt at ease to see how well Gracie listened.

"Oh, Kevin," Gracie said, grabbing Kevin's other hand and inching her chair closer to him. "I'm so sorry. That must have been hard on you."

"Yeah," Kevin said, as he moved his hand and placed it on her leg, rubbing her knee with the tips of his fingers. "It definitely wasn't an easy break-up. That's for sure. I guess all this time I've been trying to forget about it. You're the first person I've really opened up to about it. Maybe just don't tell anyone though, okay? I kind of want to keep this one a secret for as long as I can."

"Of course," Gracie said. "Cross my heart and hope to die." She made an X motion across her heart and then held out her pinky as a symbol of promise. Kevin returned the gesture, and after they kissed their hands, as was tradition to solemnize a 'pinky promise,' Kevin reached forward and gave Gracie a big hug. Other than Claire and Sam, it was the first time, in a while, he'd felt he could trust someone.

"What do you say we go for a walk?" Kevin asked. "The park's not too far from here."

"Sure," Gracie said, lacing her fingers through his. "I'd like that."

Kevin paid for their coffee and they left. The light fog made for a quaint late afternoon. He noticed that Gracie shivered as they walked, but couldn't tell if it was her nervous personality or the weather. He decided to put his jacket around her shoulders.

"Here," Kevin said, as he draped his gray bomber over her shoulders. "You seem cold."

Kevin took a moment to really look at Gracie. Despite her hyper demeanor, she was quite attractive. Everything from her left cheek dimple to her icy gray eyes, which were a stark contrast to her pure black hair, made for a harmonious mix.

"Thanks," Gracie said, smiling. She shook as if to shake the shiver out of herself. She looked up at Kevin, who was staring her. "Hey, so did I ever tell you about the owner of that coffee shop? Rumor has it he—"

Kevin seized the moment and dove in for a kiss. Part of him did it to keep her from babbling on, but another part of him did it because he liked her. They paused after the kiss to delight in the moment.

"Umm. Wow," Gracie said, pulling away while still keeping her arms wrapped around Kevin's waist. "That was unexpected. So ... umm, about the owner of the coffee shop—"

Kevin kissed her again and Gracie obliged. Gracie moved her hands up Kevin's back as the fog wrapped gentle circles around them. Something unfortunate was brewing, but to the two star-crossed lovers, nothing was purer than this moment they shared together.

Sam caught a heaping mouthful of twigs and leaves as he dove back into the bushes. He looked back up to see if anyone had noticed his futile attempt at being stealthy. No one had. He had never stalked anyone before and did his best to keep Libby from noticing him outside her dorm room window. A few hours had gone by now, and Sam was getting cold from the fog. But just as he decided to give up, he saw Libby putting on her jacket.

"That-a-girl," Sam said rubbing his hands together. "Is it finally time for a walk outside?"

Sam's hunch was correct. Libby left the building and walked past the corner, where her window rested right above Sam's secret hiding bush. It was the perfect moment of opportunity, and Sam didn't waste any time. He pulled his pants up higher and proceeded to peer into Libby's window. There seemed to be no one around as he scanned back and forth. With what burglary skills he could remember from all those spy movies he loved to watch, he slipped his library card underneath the window seal. It was just enough pressure to unlatch the lock. He lifted up the window, took one last look around, and rolled himself over the windowsill and into Libby's room.

"Ouch," Sam muttered, rubbing his side. He had fallen harder than he expected, right onto a pile of hard books.

He did a quick survey of the dorm room. It was quite clear which side of the dorm belonged to Gracie. Dozens of cat posters and kitten dolls painted the perfect picture of the hyperactive suspect. Sam got a chill in his spine from the scene.

This is totally not weird. Yeah, right. Sam thought as he judgmentally scanned the rest of Gracie's side of the room.

Then Sam started to comb through everything, being careful not to make a mess. He paused for a second and wondered. He had no idea what he was actually looking for, and even if he did, he hadn't a clue where to find it. Thinking about Gracie's personality and energy, he decided to mimic her persona and nervously look everywhere—even behind the kitten toys. After about an hour of searching, he had no luck. He was even more disappointed that his aspirations to impress Claire had failed.

"Stupid journalism club," Sam said, as he tossed a toy kitten at the wall.

Then he had one final thought. He decided to give it one last shot and began searching through Gracie's journalism books. One by one, he scoured the whole lot. But he found nothing. With failure in his eyes, he surveyed the room and did his best to tidy up. It took him a little while, but after jumping out the window—and landing much more smoothly than he had when he'd entered—he heard someone entering the dorm. He ducked behind the bushes once again and breathed a sigh of relief. He had gotten out just in time.

This relief was only temporary, however, as at that moment, Sam's phone notified him of a text. He scrambled to turn down the volume so as not to be discovered. He looked at the window and let out another sigh of relief when he saw the coast was still clear. As he looked at his phone his mouth dropped. He recognized the number all too well.

> From 617-682-7897 at 7:02pm: Naughty naughty, Sam. Too bad you'll never find what you're looking for. —Z

Sam was taken aback. If Gracie was Z, how could she have known he was in the dorm when she was on a date with Kevin? He pulled out his phone and sent a group text.

From Sam at 7:05pm: We need to meet. Tomorrow at 3pm. My dorm.

Sam brushed the leftover dirt and leaves off his clothes and looked back and forth over his shoulders. The fog hid most of the surroundings. Z was a lot more cunning than he thought.

☾

Kevin felt amazing as he took in the serenity of the campus that day. He stood outside Sam's dormitory building, taking it all in before he went inside. He felt, for once, that he had a shot at dating someone with whom he had a real connection. His mood became even brighter as he noticed Claire walking toward him, so he greeted her with a hug.

"Whoa there," Claire said. "Someone's in a good mood."

"You know?" Kevin replied as he held both of Claire's arms. "I actually am, Claire. I really am. I mean look at it. Us. Here. Such a beautiful day. Life is good isn't it?"

Claire laughed. She had never seen him like this. She hoped she had something to do with it.

"So ... I went out with Gracie yesterday," Kevin said.

Claire's hopes vanished just as quickly as they had appeared. "Oh. That's right," Claire said. "You had your date with her. How did it go?"

"It was amazing! We went to this café a little outside of Cambridge. And it was weird at first because you know how she can talk a million miles an hour, but then I felt like she really listened to me, and we just connected."

"That's great, Kevin," Claire said lowering her head.

Kevin had known her for years. He could always tell when she was lying.

"Hey, what's wrong?" Kevin asked.

"Nothing," Claire said quickly. Frantically, she changed the subject. "I'm just worried about Sam. He's been acting weird since our journalism class. I think this whole thing is making him kinda paranoid."

Kevin nodded. He knew she was referring to the text from Sam about meeting. It was the reason they were both outside his dormitory building now.

"Well, I guess we'll find out," Kevin said. He paused as he got the odd feeling they were being watched.

Kevin looked around cautiously. He noticed several people pointing in his direction. Claire noticed as well but didn't understand why. All of a sudden, a student on a skateboard cruised up to the two friends and broke the silence.

"Yo. You're Kevin?" asked the student as he flipped his skateboard up into his hands.

"Uhh, yeah, why?" Kevin said confused.

"Good stuff, man. Keep it up. You've got my vote," the student said. He dropped his board back on the sidewalk and rode off as he gave Kevin a thumbs up.

"What was that about?" Claire asked.

Kevin had no clue. "I have no idea," he said.

"Kevin! Kevin Deer!" A group of girls in the distance waved at him. "You have our vote."

"Okay, now this is getting weird," Claire said.

Kevin and Claire decided to go inside the dormitories and ignore what had just happened. They had to talk to Sam, anyway.

Unfortunately, their plan to ignore everything failed miserably. Typically the dorms were equipped with a stack of campus papers to keep the Cambridge students informed about campus events, class schedule changes, and anything else that pertained to Cambridge. Usually the contents were pretty boring, but this week's edition was different. Claire saw the front page and turned to Kevin as her jaw dropped.

"Umm, Kevin," Claire said, as she pointed at the stack of papers in the dormitory entrance.

Sam walked up with his hands on his head. "About time, guys," he said. "You're like, thirty minutes late. And all this news about you Kevin … is it really true?"

"Is what true?" Kevin asked.

Sam held up the school paper. Kevin did a double take. He blinked to refocus and make sure he was seeing the right thing. His Cupid Academy Connect profile picture was staring back at him.

☽

"How on earth did this happen?" Kevin asked. He paced back and forth in Sam's dorm.

"Gracie's a nice girl," Claire said. "I'm sure she didn't mean anything by it. Maybe it's just her personality."

Kevin looked at Sam who couldn't take his eyes off the school paper. It was horrifying. Kevin was on the front page of the school paper as an official candidate for homecoming king.

The article, written by Gracie, was even more of a shock than his profile picture—which she'd chosen to place at the center of it all. The article told of how Kevin had had a heartbreaking moment at Senior Recruitment Day, and that he'd chosen to attend Cambridge to try to make a difference in the school. It also made specific mention that he wasn't single. To top it all off, it looked like Gracie had entered him into the Spring Fling court to run for Spring Fling King.

"This title is the worst," Sam said. "Really? 'Hometown Heartbreak Vows to Be a Hero at Spring Fling?' Geez. This is bad. Here's the worst part: 'He nearly cried when he had his heart broken on Senior Recruitment Day.' This doesn't even sound like you."

"I know," Kevin said as he scanned the article over and over. "I can't believe Gracie would do this. I told her not to tell anyone. I told her that in confidence. How could I be so stupid? That's it. I'm calling her now."

"No, don't!" Sam shouted.

Kevin looked at him in disbelief. "Why not?"

"Maybe this is exactly what we need," Sam said.

Claire returned Kevin's look of confusion. "I'm not following."

"Well, that's sort of why I invited you guys over here," Sam said. "I got another text from Z. Maybe it's not a big deal. Maybe it is. But this Z mystery needs to be solved. What if something bad happens? Maybe Z is behind all of this," Sam shook the paper as if to make his point more forcefully.

"So … what are you suggesting?" Kevin asked.

"Okay, stopping the quest of the mistresses would ruin your chances at love forever right? So that's not an option. But continuing this is obviously only going to make this Z thing get worse. So the way I see it … we only have one option."

"And what's that?" Claire asked.

"We have to bring down Z," Sam said, as he took off his thick glasses and put them down on his nearby desk.

The fire in Sam's eyes made his stature braver than most people would have thought he could manage. It was enough to intrigue Kevin and Claire—not to participate, but rather to understand where his zeal was coming from.

"I feel like Gracie may be Z," Sam said.

"Here we go again," Claire scoffed, and rolled her eyes, turning her back to Sam so he wouldn't see how annoyed she was.

"You know what Claire?" Sam said to Claire's back. "Maybe you should start opening your eyes a bit more. I'm the one taking all the risks out here."

"Risks?" Claire whipped back around and put her hands on her hips. "You're kidding right?"

"Whoa, guys. C'mon, take it easy." Kevin put his hands between the two friends.

"Yeah. Risks," Sam said. "Do you even know what I had to go through to sneak into her dorm room—"

"You did what?" Kevin and Claire shouted in unison.

"That's not cool, Sam," Claire said. "You can get in huge trouble. Maybe even expelled. For what? Because you think Gracie is this cyber terrorist. Sam, I spoke with Gracie at the party that night. She is not Z. You've been paranoid ever since she's come around, and it's making you careless. You're not doing this for us. You're doing this for you."

Sam put his head down and sat down on his bed. He slumped his shoulders, and any confidence he had earlier had disappeared. Kevin felt bad for him. He knew Sam was only trying to help.

"Claire, come on. It's not a big deal," Kevin said. He tried to ease the growing tension in the room between the friends.

"No, Kevin. It's not," Claire said. She put her hand up to Kevin and continued, "You know. You guys are both selfish. This is getting too weird. I just need some space, okay?"

Claire's emotions were coming from a deeper place than Kevin could comprehend—a combination of romantic frustration and a strong desire to spend more one-on-one time with Kevin. She wasn't mad at Sam; she was mad at herself. She sighed as she looked at Kevin, and she shook her head to signal her disappointment. She felt as though she couldn't keep this up and decided to walk out the door. Kevin and Sam looked at each other. They had no idea what to do.

༄

Claire was joined by just a few other students in the media lab that afternoon. It was a stiff setting. Everyone had their oversized headphones on and their heads down as they stared at the news about Kevin on their laptops. She made herself cozy with a cup of coffee and a notebook and decided to focus on something other than Kevin for a change. Regardless of her determination to change her mindset, she couldn't help but feel guilty about how she'd stormed out of Sam's dorm room. She gave it some more thought and looked at her phone. Kevin and Sam had both sent their usual apology texts. She considered apologizing and heading back, but instead of giving in, she put her phone away and gazed around the lab. She noticed Gracie typing away like a maniac in the far corner. It would only make sense for the president of the Journalism Student Union to be here on a Friday afternoon. She decided to walk over and extend a friendly greeting.

"Looks like you're working on something pretty serious," Claire said, tapping Gracie on the shoulder.

Gracie jumped up, caught by surprise, and pulled her headphones out of her ears. She looked up at Claire, who looked frustrated and upset.

"Oh. Hi, Claire. You must be mad at me too then, huh?" Gracie asked, fiddling nervously with the cord of her headphones.

Claire knew exactly what she was talking about. Even though she had strong opinions about the article Gracie had penned, she still couldn't help but feel a bit sorry for Gracie. Her normally smooth, voluminous hair looked like it hadn't been washed in a couple of days and the bags under her eyes stood out against her fair skin. It seemed like Gracie was doing her best at her new job in the Journalism department but just didn't know how.

Gracie's eyes watered a bit. "Kevin sent me a text saying 'we need to talk,' and that he's 'upset' with me. All I wanted to do was make up for what he went through at Senior Recruitment. I just wanted him to feel special. To know that there are people here who support him and love him. Tell me the truth though. Was I wrong? He hates me, doesn't he? I knew it. Your look says it all. He totally hates me. I'm such an idiot." Gracie threw her head into her hands and started to cry.

Claire rested her hand on Gracie's shoulder. "I'm sure he doesn't hate you. Kevin's not like that. I do think you may have gone a little too far with the whole feature article thing, though. It sorta seems like you did it for *yourself*—to increase the views on the paper and maybe give you a boost as the new president?"

"Yeah. I guess maybe I did take it a bit too far," Gracie said, wiping her eyes. She sniffled and looked up at Claire. "But this is all I have, you know? Journalism and the paper. It's how I speak. It's what I know best. I don't know what I'd do without it. I didn't mean for it to come off so selfish. I just feel so misunderstood."

Claire did understand. After her last encounter with her friends, she knew what it was like to have feelings misunderstood. It felt like being trapped in a bubble that no one else could get into.

"Hey, why don't we pack up here and grab some food? You can tell me all about the perks of being in JSU," Claire said with a smile.

"Sure. I'd like that," Gracie said returning the smile. Her tears made her eyes glitter like snow on a sunny day. "Thanks, Claire. You're a good friend."

They both gathered their things and made way for the exit. Claire beamed, feeling a new sense of friendship. It felt good to be around another girl for once. Maybe this was what they both needed—to focus on media and school.

"Hey! Party girl?" said a student as he walked past Claire and Gracie. He stopped in front of Claire and smiled at her.

"Umm, I'm sorry. Do I know you?" Claire asked, confused.

"It's me. Paul. Well, you probably remember me as 'Tank.' Remember? From Laura's party a while back?"

Gracie leaned into Claire and whispered into her ear, "That's the guy who tried to talk to you and you turned him down. The no-shirt guy. Remember?"

"Oooh," Claire said, looking back at him and nodding. "I guess you look different. I didn't recognize you with a shirt on." She smirked at him and smoothed her white oxford shirt out.

Paul laughed. "Sense of humor. I like that," he said. "You can call me Paul, by the way. 'No shirt guy' only suits me some of the time." He winked at her and stuck his hand out.

"Okay then. Paul it is," Claire said returning his handshake.

"I'll see you around campus then?" Paul said flashing her another smile and a wink.

Claire couldn't help but feel somewhat flattered by the guy. She started to feel her cheeks getting hot, as she wasn't sure how to react to this unexpected attention. She looked at Gracie, who nodded happily in approval, and then Claire cleared her throat, looked back at Paul, and tried to figure out what to say.

She didn't want to come off too excited, so she just left it simple and said, "Sure."

It was just enough to walk away from. She looked back and noticed him doing the same. He waved at her, but she quickly turned around, embarrassed at having been caught. She poked Gracie and whispered, "He's looking at me." She and Gracie giggled, but Claire couldn't help but think about Kevin.

☽

Kevin listened to the charming ring of the bell tower go off multiple times and wondered where Gracie was. He wanted to resolve this matter of gossip as quickly as possible. He felt like he was losing his mind from all the campus attention in the wake of the article she had written about him. It reminded him of the paparazzi, and now he understood how celebrities felt. This kind of constant attention was enough to drive anyone mad.

"Sorry I'm late," Gracie said as she ran up to Kevin. "I got tied up with a friend."

"It's fine," Kevin said with a flat tone in his voice.

Gracie was filled with anxiety. "Kevin, I—"

"How could you do that to me?" Kevin interrupted her. "You promised me that you wouldn't tell anyone. Now the whole school knows. And to top it off you then sign me up to run for Spring Fling King? Please tell me this is a bad dream."

"Kevin ... I didn't mean to upset you ... It wasn't meant to seem like betrayal," Gracie said, as her eyes began to water. "I just ... I just really wanted your story to be heard. Everyone should hear it. It's such an amazing story. You were so brave. You're like a hero. Just think about it. All the lives it would touch. If you were to be the Spring Fling King, it could be really good for you here and—"

"Just stop. Okay? Just stop." Kevin didn't want to hear any more from Gracie. "This is crazy. I am not running for Spring Fling King. To be honest, Gracie ... I just don't know if this is working for me."

"What do you mean?" Gracie asked.

Kevin paused for a moment. "I don't know. It's just ... all of this is a bit crazy. I'm not sure if we—"

At that moment, before Kevin could finish his sentence, Gracie jumped into his arms and kissed him, leaving a smear of sparkly lip gloss on his lower lip. Kevin was lost in more ways than one.

"What was that for?" Kevin asked, stunned.

"I know, I know. I shouldn't have done that. You were mad and I just completely took advantage of the situation. I couldn't help it. I just … I really like you, Kevin. I'm sorry."

Kevin didn't know what to think. He liked Gracie and felt that she hadn't meant to hurt him with all of this. He decided to let his guard down and kiss her again, but then quickly tensed up when out of the corner of his eye he saw a student in the distance taking a photo of him.

And just as swiftly as the kiss had granted Kevin solace, the click of a camera phone and its bright flash shed light on a disturbing reality. He wondered if he was making the right choice.

"What was that?" Kevin asked and he pulled away from Gracie.

"Don't pay them any mind," Gracie said, as she turned Kevin's face back to hers. "It's probably just somebody who wants to vote for you."

He looked at Gracie, as she smiled seductively. She laced her fingers through his and rested her head on his chest. Her hair smelled like vanilla, and he wanted to take a deep breath, let go, and enjoy this moment—but his guilt kept him tied to his sense of reason. For the first time since he'd started this quest, Kevin was beginning to have doubts.

☾

Sam was a mess. It had been more than twenty-four hours, and he still refused to leave his dorm room after Claire had stormed out. He didn't even bother to turn the lights on as the evening crept in through the blinds. All he could do was think about Claire. He decided it would be best to distract himself from his frustration with the booklet of Zodiac signs and personalities that Claire had given to him and Kevin. So he held the book up to the moonlight and began reading.

It wasn't long before Sam became engrossed in every page. He was fascinated; every personality and summary of each Zodiac sign sang with tantalizing mystery—especially the Taurus. Sam remembered that Taurus was Gracie's sign, and he quickly became obsessed with understanding the meaning behind the image and summary of the Taurus mistress. He read it aloud several times to make sense of it all.

The Taurus Mistress—a sign who lives from April 20th through May 21st.
The noble side of the Taurus mistress is one with little equal.
Their horns, while sharp, could very well be just as peaceful.
Be warned. Those who tangle in a Taurus mistress' impending spell,
Should know they bring calamity with rumors to tell.

Sam looked at the Taurus illustration next to this description once more. It was a mosaic of ancient patterns, and every piece seemed to be some kind of code. There was a woman with a halo who held onto the horns of a bull. The bull's tail was the most peculiar image, as it was covered in rose thorns.

An epiphany came to Sam. He understood what the message meant, as well as the unfortunate parallel it had with Gracie. He needed to tell Kevin and Claire. He turned on his small desk lamp for the first time that evening, and after the light flooded the room he noticed a large manila envelope being slipped underneath his door. Even eerier was the shadow of a person that accompanied it.

"Who's there?" Sam asked.

The shadow scurried off as he approached the door. Sam threw open the door and quickly stepped out of his room, looking left and right, but all that remained was a lonesome hallway. He said again, "Who's there? Come out!" But was met with silence.

Sam picked up the envelope. He wrinkled his forehead as he tried to think what this could be. He peeled the sealed flap back to see what it revealed. Inside was a photo marked with red writing.

Down goes the matador. Toro. Toro.

Sam stared at the picture and shivered as goosebumps surged over him. It was a picture of Gracie kissing Kevin near the bell tower. A red circle was drawn around Kevin's face. Sam looked back down the hallway and then quickly shut his door. He locked it and then checked it again to make sure it was locked. He snapped his blinds shut and sat on his bed. He didn't have to wonder where this picture came from or who put it under his door. He knew it was Z. And as he took a moment to figure out what to do, he realized two terrible truths: The first was that Claire was right—Gracie was not Z. The second, much more alarming truth was that Z was going after Kevin somehow. Every realization made it even tougher for Sam to breathe. This problem was only getting worse. He pulled out his phone to take a picture of the envelope's contents and sent a group text to Kevin and Claire. To Kevin and Claire at 10:02 pm: "Looks like Gracie isn't Z. But I think Z may be using Gracie somehow. Look at the Taurus mistress description."

☙

Claire hurried to the media lab that evening. She was excited. It wasn't often that newcomers to the JSU were granted access on new column releases, so she appreciated that Gracie had given her the opportunity. She couldn't get to the media lab soon enough. She looked at her phone to double check the time before she walked in, and noticed the text from Sam about Z's recent message. Her excitement was quickly replaced with nervousness as she entered the lab. She took a deep breath and decided to do her best to ignore it—she wanted to have a good time at JSU.

"Hey!" Claire said, tossing her backpack onto a chair. "Sorry I'm late."

"Oh, shucks. Don't even worry about it," Gracie said, waving her hand and dismissing Claire's apology. "Everyone, this is Claire. Claire, this is Libby, Scott, Riley, and Hannah."

"Hi Claire," said the group of students in unison.

"Hi all," Claire said with a smile.

"These guys are absolutely amazing," Gracie said. "I promise to give everyone a chance to get better introduced after-ward. For now, we have stories to submit before the printing deadline. To your stations, my loves." Gracie clapped her hands in excitement.

Everyone resumed their robotic motions. The typing almost resembled the playing of a band, everyone contributing to the melody with their clicks and taps. Claire loved every bit of it.

Claire went over to speak to Gracie, who lead the relentless concert, ticking away at typos and scratching her notes down with a bright red pen onto a nearby notepad.

"So," Claire said. "How can I help?"

"Claire, shucks, you're just so sweet," Gracie said. "I'm glad you asked. Actually, how do you feel about editing our front-page story? I could really use some help here. Yes, I think it would be perfect for you. It sounds kind of like a big task, but I promise it's not! Ugh, and the story…" Gracie rolled her eyes and tied her hair back into a low ponytail as she kept talking, "You'll absolutely love it. Pinky promise you will!"

"Umm, yeah, all right," Claire said. "I'd love to do that!"

"Great. Grab a seat and I'll e-mail you the story so you can start reading it. You can make the edits directly on the story if you want, or you can print it and handwrite your edits. Whatever you feel comfortable with!" Gracie said.

Claire's nerves calmed down. She was distracted now, as she was overjoyed at the work she had just been assigned. She sat down and opened up her laptop. For the first time at Cambridge, she felt as though she had a purpose—as though she belonged. Everyone kept to themselves, but she was okay with that. It was safe. She gazed at the busy students again and then looked down to see an e-mail notification from Gracie. The anticipation made it all the more fun.

However as she soon as opened the e-mail, her anticipation and excitement turned to confusion. It was an article announcing Kevin in second place with Spring Fling King votes, right behind Paul "The Tank" Fieldman. It covered an array of personal information and included a section about Kevin's hot new dating life with Gracie—the President of JSU. There was even a picture of them kissing near the bell tower—the same picture from Sam's text message. Claire was in disbelief.

"Uhh, Gracie?" Claire asked.

"Yeah?" Gracie said.

"What's this?" Claire asked, pointing to the article she had just downloaded to her computer.

Claire pulled her laptop over to Gracie, who was only partially paying attention.

"Gracie ..." Claire said again.

"Oh that?" Gracie said. "It's just to help Kevin! I got an e-mail from some random person who took that photo of us. What do you think? Such a romantic picture, right? This will totally get Cambridge buzzing and hopefully get Kevin some more votes to get out of second place. Ugh, I think he will be so excited to win. I mean, I know he's a bit shy, but this will change that. So amazing, right?" She eagerly clapped her hands together, proud of what she had done.

"No," Claire said. "Gracie, no it's not. Does Kevin even know about this?"

"Kevin *needs* this, Claire," Gracie whispered. "Don't make a scene. He'll be fine. We talked after the first incident and I'm sure we can work it out again. He understands me. He gets what I'm doing with all of this and why."

"No, Gracie, I don't think he does," Claire said loudly.

At this point, the attention from the other four journalists begins to turn in their direction. The clicking of keyboards had stopped, and the room became tense. It was enough for Claire to close her laptop, pack her things, and head for the door.

"Where are you going?" Gracie demanded.

"Kevin is a great guy, Gracie." Claire turned around before walking out the door. "You'd know that if you weren't so busy ruining his life with all your gossip. Consider this my resignation."

☙

Kevin looked at his phone, perplexed—he had just silenced the vibrations again. It was his eleventh missed call from Gracie, and he had no intention of picking up. The most recent article had been released, and Kevin could only wallow in embarrassment and regret. He felt betrayed and couldn't stand the thought of being around anyone, especially Gracie. As he looked at the view from the observatory that night, he questioned it all. Every star seemed to know its place in the universe; he wished he could be so lucky, and wondered if everything had been a mistake. Susan, Laura, now Gracie, and the rest of the unknown Zodiac mistresses—it all caused a deep disturbance in his reflective thought. These thoughts were so relentless and distracting that Kevin almost missed the sound of footsteps from a nearby observer. He looked to the other side of the observatory roof and saw a girl who seemed as though she could relate to his current state. She looked back at him and gave him a quick smile to acknowledge that she knew he was there. Kevin felt she had a sense of understanding. Perhaps she had the answers to his predicament. He felt as though there was a strange connection; it felt like he was being pulled in her direction. But he figured it was just his gentlemanly instincts—he couldn't ignore a lady.

"They say that you can see a lot more shooting stars from this side," said the mystery girl. "Maybe I can make a wish before the night is over."

"Do you come here a lot?" Kevin asked.

"Probably more than I should," said the girl. She followed her response with a nervous laugh.

Kevin forced himself to laugh a bit as well. He needed to.

"I know who you are," said the girl. "You seem like you're up here for a reason."

"Yeah. Seems like a lot of people know who I am these days," Kevin said and sighed. "Wish it was under better circumstances."

"I guess that's why I come here from time to time," the girl said. "To be invisible. To see what most people take for granted."

Kevin looked at the girl and she returned his gaze. Her big, round eyes were like melted pools of caramel candy. They looked back at the view and understood each other. In a subtle way, the constellations seemed to echo their sentiments. It was a captivating stillness.

"What do you think I should do?" Kevin asked.

"You're asking me?" said the girl. "I'm not really the best person to ask for advice."

"Yeah, well … I think any advice would help at this point," Kevin said. He put his head down.

The girl looked at Kevin with sympathy. "Maybe … maybe it's just like tonight," she said. "You start off by trying to escape from something, and regardless, you end up coming into contact with it anyway."

"So you mean you're up here trying to avoid people too?" Kevin said.

"Yeah, I am," she said, pulling the sleeves of her navy cashmere sweater over her knuckles "But I guess sometimes things don't always go as planned. But maybe that's a good thing. Maybe you just go with it."

The girl's advice was enough to clear a path through all of the confusion. Glimpses of a solution became visible through clouds of uncertainty. It felt like refreshing waves brushed on the shores of his mind.

He broke this train of thought as the girl began to gather up her things to leave. "Uhh ... wait," Kevin said, touching her arm. "I don't even know your name."

The girl smiled. Only a handful of people ever really cared to ask her name, much less anything else about her. She let her guard down and relaxed.

"It's Libby," she said with a shy smile, so as not to expose her braces.

"So will I ever see you around here again, Libby?" Kevin asked.

Libby continued toward the exit stairwell of the observatory. Kevin looked on, fascinated by her aloof, mysterious vibe. She took another look at the view of the constellations they had bonded over and then looked back at Kevin. She tapped her fingers in the air as she waved at him.

"Bye, Kevin."

Kevin, although disappointed at her exit, felt he understood why she'd left the way she did. Given the state he was in, he couldn't offer much more than that himself. He sat down and continued to look at the sky. A gust of appreciation came over him, and he felt he finally knew what to do next. He decided he was going to run for Cambridge Spring Fling King.

☾

Kevin and Sam were speechless. Everything about the school gymnasium that evening sang notes of a neon wonderland. The theme was "Disco Dance Party." Ceiling projectors cast neon matrix images and lasers on the floor, sparkling white cloths and glittery centerpieces complemented the furniture, and the main stage illuminated everything with school nostalgia.

Even with all this splendor, there were several things that distracted the two friends from the grand event. First, there was Gracie, who had walked by Kevin about a dozen times without saying a word. It was more than clear to Kevin that she was still upset about their breakup. He felt like he clammed up awkwardly every time she came near him. Then there was Claire, who was at the dance with a date—Paul "The Tank" Fieldman. It was Sam's worst nightmare, and a chemistry neither Kevin or Sam could understand. They did their best to be cordial as they walked up to say hello to their friend.

"Look at what the cat dragged in," said Paul, as he wrapped his arms around Claire and planted a kiss on her temple.

"Hey, guys," Kevin said. "Paul, good luck tonight," Kevin tried to break the tension between him and his Spring Fling King competition.

"I'm going to get us some drinks, Claire," Paul said. He proceeded to bump shoulders with Kevin as he walked away.

Claire brushed her hair to the side. She was a stunning sight. The typical tomboy had changed her style for the night—she wore a tight rose gold sequin dress that exposed one shoulder and clung tightly to her hips. Her dark hair had been curled and combed over to the side of her exposed shoulder. She had swiped a matching rose gold powder across her eyelids, and the projector lights caught the glimmer every time she closed her eyes. But Kevin and Sam could only marvel at the fact that she was accompanied by such a barbaric specimen of a human.

"So . . . Paul, huh?" Kevin asked.

"What's that supposed to mean?" Claire retorted. "And what's that look for? What? Was I just supposed to come alone to this thing?"

"I'm just surprised he wore a shirt," Kevin said.

"You guys are idiots," Claire said and pulled her dress down towards her knees.

"You look nice," Kevin said. "It's different for you, but really nice."

Claire's did her best to keep from blushing. She wished she could put that moment on replay. She knew better than that, however, and changed the subject.

"So ... kinda lame music, right?"

"Yeah. They're definitely lacking some good dance electro," Sam said.

He paused after he spoke. Claire noticed as well: It was the first time they had spoken to each other since Claire had stormed out of his dorm. Kevin recognized the awkward moment and decided to let his two friends work it out.

"I'm going to get up to the main stage, guys," Kevin said, as he adjusted his suit jacket and smoothed out his hair. "They should be announcing the winner soon."

"Okay, good luck, Kevin," Claire said. She picked a piece of lint off his jacket and flicked it away.

Kevin nodded and walked away. Claire turned her attention back to Sam and smiled awkwardly. Sam returned the look and tried to show her he cared about her, smiling through his eyes. They both knew without anything having to be said.

"Well, I should get going too," Sam said, adjusting his glasses.

"Hey, Sam?" Claire touched his arm. "Hey, you were right. You were right about Gracie. I mean, even though she wasn't Z, there is definitely something weird about her. I just thought that I had finally made a friend who was a girl, you know?"

Sam was elated. Claire's touch felt like electricity buzzing through his body. "It's okay," he said. "I guess we're lucky it didn't get any worse than that, right?"

"Definitely," Claire said. "Friends?" She stuck out her fist.

"Friends," Sam said returning the fist bump.

"Didn't fist bumping die along with bow ties?" Paul said, frowning at Sam's attire. He handed Claire a soda. "Hey, so they should be announcing the winner shortly. Wanna squeeze in a dance?"

Claire looked at Sam, who had his head down. She felt his embarrassment as he awkwardly adjusted his baby-blue bow tie.

"Actually, Paul ... I promised this dance to Sam," Claire said, handing back the drink.

Sam looked up in shock. "Me?" he asked, pointing to his chest.

"Yeah. Come on!" Claire said, grabbing his arm and leading him to the dance floor. "Let's show Cambridge what we're made of."

Paul rolled his eyes. "Whatever."

Sam felt on top of the world. Claire felt she'd stood up justly for her friend. They both felt the urge to dance.

❧

Kevin took a deep breath as the Spring Fling event coordinator prepared to make the announcement on stage. He hadn't been this nervous since his Senior Recruitment day speech. Being up on stage again was giving him flashbacks to that moment and now he couldn't stop thinking about the ordeal with Susan. All he could see were the muddled faces of students looking on in curiosity. The flashing lasers and lights made everything seem like a blurry dream. Kevin looked over at Paul, who scowled back at him.

The student moderator glanced at the card and said, "And this year's Spring Fling King is ... ." Kevin saw her look at her flashcard one more time before she continued, "Umm, wow. It's Kevin Deer." She waved her arm toward Kevin.

Kevin couldn't believe it. He had won. He walked up to the student moderator and waited to hear who the students had selected as Spring Fling Queen.

"We love you, Kevin!" shouted a group of students. Others cheered to echo their enthusiasm.

"And, for Spring Fling Queen, the winner is ... Gracie Willows!" the moderator announced.

Everyone looked around for Gracie, but she was nowhere to be seen.

"Gracie Willows?" the moderator repeated.

Kevin looked around, only to see shoulder shrugs and hear whispers of confusion from the crowd of students. He began to blame himself; he was the reason Gracie was not accepting the award, and he felt bad that their relationship had ended the way it did. He found Sam and Claire in the crowd, and they looked just as confused.

"Well, everyone," announced the moderator. "I guess ..."

Before she could continue, static noise filled the room, and a video began to play on the projector screen behind the main stage. Kevin turned around to see Gracie on the screen. It looked as though the footage playing was live. Her black hair was knotted in a frizzy ball on top of her head, and her eyes looked cold and dull. The puffy bags under her eyes gave away that she had been crying for quite some time.

"Hello everyone. Students," Gracie said. "If you're watching this, it's probably because you've noticed I'm not there right now. I refuse to accept this award. First of all, as you may or may not know ... Kevin and I are no longer a couple. He dumped me. But let me tell you why he dumped me. You see, Kevin, while he may seem so nice on the outside ... he's actually someone who uses people. "

Kevin was in shock. He looked back at the audience. It was like Senior Recruitment day all over again.

"Can someone cut the feed?" the moderator asked into the microphone, motioning to the tech crew at the back of the gymnasium.

"Kevin Deer … is not the winner of Spring Fling." Gracie pointed into the camera as if pointing directly at Kevin. "You see? Look. The voting codes. I have them right here." Gracie held a piece of paper close to her camera to show a collection of numbers underneath Kevin's name and another collection of numbers underneath Paul's name. Gracie took the paper away to show her face again and kept talking. "Kevin encouraged me to rig the votes so we could be king and queen together. All of it. The stories, the rumors, the truths, my love for him … he used me for it all. Just like he used you guys."

Kevin felt everything go silent—not because there was actual silence, but because his mind had muted the sound to block out the trauma that was happening. The Taurus had just admitted her love for him. Everything that followed happened in slow motion.

He had a strange sense that something was about to happen, and turned to his right in time to duck a punch from Paul "Tank" Fieldman. Paul hit the moderator by accident, and in retaliation, the moderator pushed Paul off the stage. Paul's teammates jumped on stage, rushing for Kevin, but the school faculty engaged just in time, holding them back. Kevin ran off the stage but quickly fell to the ground after being hit by a random punch. Students began to pounce on one another like wild animals. All he could do was watch everything go up in flames. He thought about Z's last message before he passed out.

"Down goes the matador. Toro. Toro."

Kevin had never seen so much school spirit. Each wooden wall of the dean's office was covered in Cambridge emblems, banners, newspaper articles, and tapestries made with the school color, navy blue. He marveled at the décor with one eye open. He couldn't remember how he'd gotten here, but he figured that somebody had escorted him straight from Spring Fling. His other eye was covered with an ice pack. It had closed up, and he winced in pain when he carefully touched his eyelid to try to assess the damage.

"Mr. Deer," said an authoritative voice.

Kevin focused his attention on the Cambridge dean, whose frown said everything about his disapproval of the Spring Fling fiasco.

"Mr. Deer," said Dean Alex Keller again. "I am quite shocked. Normally the winner of the Charter Scholarship doesn't carry so much drama with him. And I don't have to tell you that fighting on campus can be grounds for expulsion."

"Sir, I can explain," said Kevin.

"No need. I have everything I believe I need to sort out this matter," Dean Keller said. "Lucky for you, you had a friend who cleared up everything. So you're free to go with a warning. Your friend, on the other hand, well, they didn't make out so lucky."

"Which friend?" Kevin said, disheartened that somebody had taken the fall for him. He knew that while he may not have been the direct cause of this particular fight, his journey to find the Zodiac mistresses was at the root of the madness.

Dean Keller smiled. "I've never been one to gossip, Mr. Deer. I'm sure you'll find out soon enough. Keep in mind that I'm still deeply disappointed, so I expect to see you turn things around. Now, you're free to go back to your dorm. Have a good night."

Kevin walked out of the office with a mixture of gratitude and guilt. Sam and Claire were waiting for him in the lobby. Their eyes were filled with hope as they stood up to greet him.

"How did it go?" Claire asked.

"Fine, I guess," Kevin said, still in a daze.

"You definitely don't seem fine," Claire said.

"It's just … well, Dean Keller said a 'friend' explained what had happened and they took the fall for everything," Kevin said. "I just wish I knew who it was."

Claire and Sam glanced at each other and shrugged. Just like Kevin, they had no clue who it could be.

"It's been a long day … and night," Kevin said, and he put his arms around both his friends. "What do you say we all get out of here, yeah?"

"You don't have to ask me twice," Sam said, patting Kevin on the back.

As the trio left the lobby, Claire noticed a familiar face in the hall. It was Gracie, and she was sitting on a bench, kicking her feet back and forth and reading something on her laptop; her hands were shaking as she scrolled up and down. Claire knew at that moment who Kevin's honest hero 'friend' was. She needed to get her questions answered.

"Hey, guys," Claire said. "I'll catch up with you later."

Kevin and Sam went on as Claire walked toward the occupied bench. There sat Gracie with her head low, buried in her laptop.

"What made you do it?" Claire asked, and plopped herself next to Gracie.

Gracie looked over at Claire, surprised. She took a moment to gather herself. "You were right, Claire," she said. "Kevin's a great guy. He didn't deserve that. I guess ... I guess I just went a little crazy. I guess that's what love does to a person sometimes. I'm sure you know better than anyone."

Claire understood what she meant, and they returned a warm look of respect. Once again, Claire saw past all of Gracie's antics. She was just misunderstood.

"Thank you," Claire said and she gave Gracie a tight squeeze. She knew it would be her last time seeing her friend at the school.

As Claire walked away, Gracie called out to her. "Claire?"

"Yeah?" Claire turned around to see that Gracie had shut her laptop.

"Be careful, okay?" Gracie warned. "Whoever it is, they don't like you guys."

"Wait, what? Who?" Claire said, puzzled.

Gracie looked at Claire and the same bit of chill gripped them both.

"Z," Gracie said.

That halted any celebratory thoughts that Claire might have had. The room seemed to be quieter than it had been before they spoke. All Claire could do was remain frozen.

There was a lump in her throat that caused her to be mute. "Who...?" was all she could manage to get out.

"Z," Gracie repeated. "Remember when I told you that somebody sent me that photo of me and Kevin kissing? The one I used in the newspaper? Well, that came from 'Z.' At first..."

Claire cut Gracie off, "Why wouldn't you tell me then? You didn't think that was the least bit suspicious...?!"

"Claire," Gracie continued. "I didn't. I didn't even know you knew a 'Z' and I figured it was harmless—like the celebrity paparazzi. Photos come from anyone, anytime, anywhere. I just...I guess I let the journalist in me brush any weirdness aside. Anyways, before the dance, I got another message from 'Z.' This time, it *was* weird. They said, 'Kevin used you to continue a quest—a conquest—of love. He just wants to bring you down so he can move on to a new lover. You would be smart to bring him down and ruin him before he does it to you.' I didn't know what to do. And that's why I made that video. But..."

"Stop! I've heard enough" Claire put her hands over her ears. "This is too freaky and I don't want to hear any more; I just want this to stop."

Gracie gave Claire a hug, slipped a piece of paper into the palm of Claire's hand, and said, "Just be careful, Claire. I don't know who they are. I truly don't, but please be careful." Claire wiped the tears from her cheek, further smearing her soft eyeshadow, then hurried off to try and catch up with Sam and Kevin. Claire knew she had to tell them immediately.

CLAIRE, SAM, KEVIN, AND
DEAR READERS,

Z SENT ME A SECRET LINK
TO DOWNLOAD MY OWN COPY
OF KUBO'S MAGICAL BOOK AND
I'VE KEPT IT WITH ME.

YOU SHOULD DO IT TOO; IT
MAY CONTAIN CLUES TO HELP
YOU UNDERSTAND EACH UNIQUE
ZODIAC SIGN.

VISIT http://bit.ly/2VRZ82I
TO DOWNLOAD YOUR OWN
COPY!
XO,
GRACIE

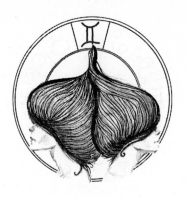

CHAPTER IV

—THE GEMINI WITH THE GIFT OF GLOOM—

Gemini: May 21ˢᵗ–June 21ˢᵗ

The Gemini, a loyal air sign, is often seen as fun and adventurous but often plays the role of two souls. It is believed that every good human has two separate personalities, but most of us can not access both sides and so, we are either one way or we are the other. It is only the Gemini mistress who can balance both the unstable, unreliable personality with their structured, loveable side. The Gemini mistress despises the feeling of boredom and as such, can often stir up adventure and emotion to set a change of pace. Passionate, curious, adaptable, the Gemini will pull Kevin and his friends into adventure, but along the way, they will have to navigate between complete opposites to find a happy medium.

Kevin, Claire, and Sam sat in Sam's dorm for what seemed like hours. Everything over the last two months just wasn't adding up. Their chart of suspects was filling up, yet no one seemed to be a close connection to Z. One by one they reviewed the list of names and scanned the images.

"Okay," Claire said. "So ... we have Professor Kubo. Dead. Laura. At a wellness center. Professor Thompson. Quit teaching after Laura tried to kill him. Gracie. Expelled and actually warned us about Z, but didn't know who they are."

"What about Paul?" Sam asked. "Or better yet, 'the Tank-slash-jerk.'"

"Cool it, half-pint," Claire said giving Sam a shove. "If you remember, it was your idea to only list people directly linked to either Kubo or Z. Paul hasn't had any connections at all, so far. I need you to get with the program, okay? Thanks."

"I don't know. I get this feeling that you really like the guy, so maybe you're blind to his connection to the whole matter." Sam started to tease Claire, "You probably say 'Oh, Tank. Woe is me. Please take your shirt off and rescue me.'"

Claire rolled her eyes and landed a solid punch on Sam's shoulder. As funny as his antics were, they were not far from the truth. She did feel like her feelings were growing stronger for Paul. She had forgiven him for trying to punch Kevin and she was slowly peeling back his tough exterior— to her, he was actually, a really nice guy. She looked over at Kevin, who shook his head laughing at the other two. She wondered if any of this made him jealous in the slightest. She wished it did.

"All right," Kevin said, interrupting their flirtation. "I don't get it. Something's just not making sense with all this. I feel like no matter who we really analyze, they put us back to square one. Even with all the texts we've received and everything that's happened, it still feels like we've got *literally* nothing."

Kevin sat back in frustration. He knew he was lucky to have encountered the first two mistresses thus far, but his hunch was that Z would only make it tougher as he continued his journey to find love. With ten more mistresses to go, this could get more and more dangerous. It was almost as if Z knew their every move before they even made it.

"That's it," Kevin mumbled to himself.

"What's it?" Sam asked.

"That's it," Kevin said. "Z knows our moves. We're followed, messaged, photographed. Z has all this access. We can use it to our advantage, right? We can set a trap."

"Ehh, it's not a terrible idea," Sam said. "This psycho will mess up at some point. Let's force it to happen sooner rather than later. What's your plan?"

"It's got to be something that brings him or her out into the open," Kevin said.

"Oh!" Claire exclaimed. "I think I know. What about this?"

Claire pulled out a crumpled flyer from her bag and smoothed it out on Sam's desk for everyone to read. In two days there was going to be a viewing party at the observatory so that the students could see the comet Achlys. This would be perfect. They might finally be able to catch Z.

❧

The sparkling night sky made for thoughtful conversation as students gathered in the observatory to see the much-anticipated comet. The top of the observatory was full of personality that night. Every person showed a glow of excitement that filled the surrounding void. Kevin, Claire, and Sam scanned every face that walked by, smiling in order to conceal their covert spy operation. And yet, despite their diligence, nothing stood out as out of the ordinary—except for one thing. Kevin noticed *her* just as he'd noticed her before. Libby was there, and he was getting lost in her big eyes, just as he had on the first night he met her at the observatory. It was enough to keep him distracted from the task at hand.

"Kevin? Kevin?" Claire asked, snapping her fingers in front of his face.

Kevin shook his head to clear out his trance.

"You seemed like you lost yourself for a bit," Claire said.

"Yeah. Sorry … about that," Kevin said.

Sam interrupted. "Hey! Any sign of you-know-who?"

"Nope. Not for me," Claire said, and shrugged her shoulders.

"Yeah. Same," Kevin said.

"Maybe we should split up. Divide and conquer. The whole Scooby-Doo and the gang thing," Claire said.

"Good grief," Sam said, rolling his eyes.

Claire punched his shoulder. "Shut up! It worked for them." She took another quick glance around the crowd. "Don't forget to take a picture with your phone if you see anything weird." The trio went off in separate directions.

Students looked on in awe and pointed at the first glimpse of the comet. Kevin decided to take a quick break from tracking down Z and joined in on the admiration.

"It's amazing isn't it?" Kevin recognized the soft, shy voice that had spoken to him. He looked over to see Libby standing next to him and looking at the comet. She looked even more beautiful up close. Her large, puppy-dog eyes gave her a look of sweet innocence, and her olive skin glittered in the night sky. Kevin couldn't place the reason why, but her mystery was like a magnet. He was in a trance anytime he looked at her.

"Didn't anyone ever teach you that staring is rude?" Libby asked, not taking her gaze off the comet.

Kevin cleared his throat and looked back up to the comet. He was embarrassed. Libby let out a small laugh.

"You were staring at me earlier too," Libby said. "From across the observatory. You can always just say 'hi' you know? I promise I won't bite." She kept her gaze on the sky.

"Oh ... umm, yeah," Kevin said. "I guess I was tied up looking for someone with my friends."

There was a pause, but it wasn't an awkward pause. Kevin and Libby enjoyed their reunion in the silence.

"It's the goddess of misery," Libby said.

"What is?" Kevin asked confused.

"The comet's name. Achlys." Libby pointed to the comet. "She was known as the goddess of misery. In fact, she was so gruesome, they say she was even put on the shield of one of the mightiest Greek heroes—Hercules. He used it to put fear into his adversaries. It's funny how they can name something so pretty after something so ugly."

"Interesting. I never knew that," Kevin said.

"Ehh, nothing you can't learn from a bunch of Internet blogs," Libby said.

Kevin laughed. He looked at Libby, who was looking back at him. In a strange way, it was almost as if she was looking to see if he was really there. Kevin wanted to lose himself in that look but found himself distracted by a familiar looking artifact dangling from her neck.

Libby noticed. "What? This?" Libby asked pulling the gold pendant on her necklace up to give him a closer look.

"Huh?" Kevin said dazed.

"Come on. Don't tell me you don't know what this is," Libby teased. "It's the symbol for Gemini. My dad gave it to me. It's my Zodiac sign." She traced the lines that had been etched on her pendant.

❧

Claire spent a few moments scanning the crowd before she got lost in its purpose. She eventually looked up to see what all the commotion was about. It was a marvelous sight. The distant, emerald and purple comet stood out against the starry background. It was an image that would be difficult for anyone to forget. It was priceless. As Claire fell in love with this novelty, she thought about the emptiness she felt. She had nobody to share this moment with. She glanced around the observatory roof to find Kevin. Even though she knew she couldn't, she had this strong desire to grab his hand and share this view with him.

Her musings soon came to a halt as she finally spotted him from across the deck, and saw that he wasn't alone. Claire's stomach churned as she saw Kevin reach for the girl's necklace. She ventured off back into the crowd.

"You look lost," said Paul.

Claire didn't acknowledge the remark. She chose to focus on the sky instead.

"Hey," Paul asked, taking Claire's hand. "You okay?"

Claire wasn't ignoring him at this point. She just didn't know how to answer that question.

"Well ... you look great," Paul insisted.

"Thank you," Claire said. She looked at her shoes and smiled, still unsure how to accept Paul's loving advances and compliments.

"And there she is," Paul teased, squeezing her hand tighter. "There's that smile I love."

Claire did her best to fight off more smiles. She wanted Kevin to notice how much attention she was getting.

"You wanna go walk around?" Paul asked.

"Sure," Claire said.

They walked away as she took one final look back at Kevin for the evening. He was nowhere to be seen. She decided to let it go for now.

"So what made Paul Fieldman show up to an astronomy event?" Claire asked Paul, as they walked through the observatory. "I thought you hated things like this."

Paul laughed. "Come on. Really?" he asked.

"No really," Claire said. "I believe the term you used was that this was 'too nerdy' for your taste."

"Well ... if you must know, I'm actually trying to find my sister," Paul said, doing another quick survey of the roof. "I thought she might be up here. I'm trying to keep her from doing anything stupid."

"Oh," Claire said. "I didn't know you had a sister."

"Yep," Paul said, wrapping his arms around Claire. "There's a lot you don't know about me, Claire."

Claire felt a bit awkward. "Imagine that," she said with a slight laugh.

"Claire," Paul said. "I like you. There's no need to be so uptight, you know?"

"I'm not up—" Claire started to say.

Before she could finish, Paul had already planted his lips on hers. She took a moment to decide whether she liked it or not. She did, but she still decided to keep him on his toes with a gentle slap.

"Okay. And what was that for?" Paul asked holding the side of his face.

"You just ... you should have asked first," Claire said, blushing.

◦))

Sam was focused that evening. Part of it was because he felt he had something to prove to his friends. The other part of it was that he wanted to impress Claire. Both parts came from a place of genuine bravery. He scanned the crowd while monitoring his friends. A wave of frustration came over him as he saw Kevin losing focus to someone he recognized—Libby. He peered through the silhouettes of students all pointing upward, paying close attention to be sure that she was not a suspect. After deliberating for a while, he decided there was nothing suspicious about Libby or her surroundings, and so he moved on.

He found Claire. This encounter was a far more disappointing one, something he wished he hadn't seen: Paul, or as Sam called him 'Tank,' had his arms wrapped around Claire like an octopus's tentacles. It took all his self-control not to blurt out something inappropriate. Instead, he sat and watched Paul kiss Claire. This brought Sam's spirit to an all-new low. He turned around before seeing Claire's playful slap, which might have boosted his spirits a little bit if he'd seen it. He decided to give up his hunt for Z and instead went to peer over the edge of the observatory deck. There were fewer people around there. Even so, he still managed to stumble over a stranger.

"I'm so sorry," Sam said. He did his best to help her pick up her purse, which he had kicked over.

"It's fine, really," the lady said. She quickly began shoving her belongings back into her purse.

Sam let out a sigh and looked back toward where Claire had been. He felt the evening was bringing him a series of bad luck.

"If I didn't know any better, I'd say you weren't too excited about being here," said the lady. Her tight dress showed her confidence as she pushed her shoulders back.

Sam glanced to his left and his right to be sure she was talking to him. The lady giggled.

"You're adorable," she said as she stuck out her hand. "I'm Doctor Eva."

"Uhh ... nice to meet you," Sam said. He shook her hand and was surprised somebody this beautiful was talking to him. *Could this be Z*, he thought. *No, couldn't be. Z wouldn't be so obvious.*

"So ... are you catching any action on this side?" Eva teased.

"I wish," Sam said peering over the deck. He tore off small bits of the event flyer, balled them up and tossed them over the railing. "This event is lame. Everyone's either off looking at that stupid comet or off kissing some other guy right in front of you."

"I see," Eva said as she leaned over the deck as well. "You know ... I never liked these kinds of events either. I come because of my husband but ... well, let's just say he tends to get lost in the crowd."

"Yeah. Totally blows," Sam said. He threw another small wad of paper over the deck.

"You are just too adorable," Eva said. She put her hand on Sam's shoulder. Her fingers were long and graceful, adorned with beautiful thin, gold rings stacked one on top of another.

Sam, who had never received any attention of the sort other than his Spring Fling dance with Claire, noticed the faint touch. He looked over at Eva and realized how attractive she was. She looked older, but not much older than the seniors at Cambridge. He was speechless, nervous, and captivated all at once.

"What's your name, darling?" Eva asked.

"Sam," he said with a nervous tone. "My name's Sam."

"Well, Sam ... I run a counseling center here on campus for students who need academic and, well, moral support," Eva said as she handed Sam her card. "You can stop by my office anytime."

Sam looked at her card. Although he couldn't be sure there was a mutual attraction, he held this encounter close. It was the first time any woman had given him a phone number. His earlier impression of his luck that evening changed.

"I'd better get going," Eva sighed. "Have to make sure the old ball and chain is happy." She ran her delicate fingers through her honey blonde hair, shook it out to the side and gave Sam another smile.

"Bye, Sam," Eva said.

Sam was speechless again. He watched as she disappeared. For the first time in a long time, he felt a small boost of confidence. He might have not found any clues leading to Z, but to him, this connection was much more meaningful.

☾

The following day, Kevin stepped out of a yellow cab, grateful and excited. It was his first summer night out on the town, and he was sharing the experience with Libby. After meeting for the second time at the observatory, both felt a connection that they decided to pursue. Libby had invited Kevin to enjoy the first warm summer night with her and suggested they go to a local dance club. He gave her a call to let her know he had arrived at the address she had texted him earlier that day. Libby squealed over the phone, which confirmed to him that she was also excited about their planned rendezvous.

Kevin thought for a second about why he had kept this a secret from Claire and Sam. He wondered if he was doing the right thing, and thought about sending them a quick text to alert them of his plans. But he quickly decided against it and shoved his phone back in his pants pocket. All he wanted was a normal date for once. No Z, no pressure, just a night out with a Gemini who he thought to be amazing.

He could see Libby walking toward him. She had on red velvet shoes with heels so skinny, he wondered how she stayed balanced and upright. Her tight black crop-top and low-rider jeans exposed a small tattoo on her ribs and a sparkling emerald stone belly ring. Kevin almost didn't recognize her without her Cambridge uniform—he didn't realize she had this wild side to her.

"So what do you think?" Libby said as she walked up and pointed at the club. "Absolutely awesome right?"

Kevin followed her hand to see that she was pointing at a neon sign just above his head: CLUB PHOENIX.

Neither her revealing outfit or the club was something he was used to, but maybe it was just what he needed.

"Umm, Libby … I don't think we can get in here. We're underage," Kevin whispered.

"You're so sweet, Kevin. But you also worry too much," Libby said, playfully poking him in the chest. "Leave this up to me, will you? God, I'm so pumped for this!"

Kevin was a bit thrown off as Libby gave him a rough punch to the chest. In their previous encounters, Libby had been more reserved and timid. Now it was like he was meeting her for the first time. He remembered what he read about Gemini having split personalities, but he figured she was just excited for the club and the start of summer, so he let the thought go.

As they walked up to the entrance, Kevin realized he didn't have any cash left after the cab ride. The bouncer didn't seem as though he handed out favors either. His concern was interrupted by a confident and bubbly Libby.

"Mozzy!" Libby said. "How are you? Tell us, is the party inside crazy or what?"

"Do I know you?" Mozzy said, confused.

"Of course you do," said Libby, glancing at Kevin. She looked back at Mozzy, who still had no clue. "Oh come on. I was here just last week. You signed me up for VIP. Remember?"

"Your name?" Mozzy said.

"Libby. Last name Fieldman," Libby said.

Kevin recognized the last name all too well. He did a double take at Libby as if he didn't recognize her. He hoped she wasn't related to his Spring Fling enemy, Paul Fieldman.

"Okay, yeah. My bad. Your name's right here," Mozzy said, as he placed a check next to a name and put away his clipboard. He pulled the velvet rope back and invited them in. "You kids stay safe, and have fun."

Libby grabbed Kevin's arm and rushed in. Kevin's reserve kept him from matching her pace. After learning her last name, he wondered even more if this was a good idea.

"Fieldman?" Kevin asked. "Is there some relation to Paul Fieldman?"

"My brother," Libby answered while checking in her leopard-patterned faux fur coat. "Well, half. Same dad, different mom. We never talk about it, though."

"You know he's like my arch enemy, right?" Kevin said.

"Relax," Libby said grabbing Kevin's cheeks. "What happens in Club Phoenix *stays* in Club Phoenix."

Kevin was charmed. He relaxed his face as his tension disappeared. Her eyes were filled with intrigue and adventure, and her revealing outfit made him feel like they were just here to have fun. She smiled when she realized he understood and led him toward the dance floor. The music pulsated through their bodies. It was a steady beat that made everything go numb, and there were enough peaks in the rhythm to build up constant excitement. The flashing lights camouflaged everyone's features. People of all shapes and sizes lost themselves on the dance floor. The DJ appeared just as lost. It was ecstasy at its finest.

"Come on! Dance with me!" Libby said.

Kevin watched as she pulled her hair loose from the tight bun on top of her head. Her copper brown hair fell in waves across her shoulders. Every twist and turn she made pushed her deeper into the music. He enjoyed watching but shied away from trying to do the same thing.

"Are you going dance shy on me?" Libby whispered as she slid up close to him.

At this point, Kevin was mesmerized. Libby ran her hands through her hair, and her wild waves tickled Kevin's cheeks as she danced closer and closer to him. He soon found patterns in the music that he could follow to work out some kind of dance move. Against his will, his body volunteered a simple two-step motion. Libby smiled and increased her movement in approval. Her hair began to fly everywhere and Kevin assumed this meant he was dancing decently now. He looked around for confirmation. There were a few head nods and thumbs poking up. He obliged and increased his intensity. He wanted to grab Libby by the waist and just dance with her. But he shied away and kept dancing. Soon, another guy walked up to Libby.

"Hey there," Libby said to the stranger.

She danced with the new suitor as intensely as she had with Kevin. Kevin felt alone. He looked around for those same nods and thumbs but was met with nothing. His speed suddenly slowed down. He watched as Libby smiled from the whispers of her new dance partner. The scene made him feel like the smallest person in the room. Libby noticed Kevin had stopped moving and danced up to him.

"Are you okay?" Libby shouted over the music.

Kevin didn't want to seem upset. He wanted to believe that this wasn't the same person he met on the deck of the observatory.

"I'm going to go get a drink really quickly with my new friend," Libby said, pointing back at her new dance partner. "You'll be okay right?" Libby asked.

Kevin nodded. It was all he could do. He watched as they scurried off in the crowd. He began to worry when they didn't return after a while, and he decided to go find the girl he'd first met. He walked around the bar but didn't see them there. His frustration grew. Finally, after searching the dance floor and a few empty corridors, he found them in a hallway where the lines for the bathroom were just as crowded as the club. Libby looked like she was attempting to push the guy off of her, and he appeared to be aggressively shoving himself closer to her. Kevin mustered up what courage he could and grabbed the guys arm. "Hey, buddy," he shouted.

Libby looked shocked but relieved. Kevin was even more shocked when the guy twisted his arm and slammed him into the wall. Club security caught on quickly and surrounded them. As they put his arms behind his back and led him toward an exit, all Kevin could do was look back at Libby with disappointment.

☽

Claire peered at her computer screen in deep thought. Gracie's warning about Z kept playing over and over in her head. She looked around the library and felt comforted that there were more people in there than usual. It was time for their spring quarter exams, so students were flipping through textbooks, reading flashcards over and over, and quizzing each other in preparation. It reminded her just how much she had to study herself. She opened up her books and began to digest the information in them. With all the commotion she had been going through with Kevin and Sam, it was easy to let the idea of school get away from her. She decided she would stay away from distractions for the time being.

"Hey there, gorgeous," said a male voice in front of her.

Claire looked up over her computer monitor to see Paul holding a rose in his mouth as a romantic gesture. She ignored it and went back to reading. It was her way of showing him he would have to try harder than that.

"Look, babe. I'm sorry, okay?" Paul exclaimed. "I didn't mean to cancel on you the other night, but I had a family emergency."

"Sure," Claire said with her head still down. She refused to give him eye contact.

"Hey," Paul said as he plopped the rose down onto her keyboard. "I like you. A lot. What's it gonna take to show you that?"

"How about honesty, for starters," Claire said. "You can't just say that we're going to hang out and then blow me off. Or say that you're into me then ignore me for days on end. I'm not that kind of girl Paul. I won't keep coming back. Look, I'm not mad, but I'm not interested in being treated like a chess piece in someone's dating game."

"I didn't lie, okay," Paul insisted. "Claire—my sister's literally been going crazy. I've had to watch out for her. She doesn't really have anyone else."

"And you expect me to believe that?" Claire asked.

"You don't have to," Paul said. "But it's the truth."

For the first time, Claire looked into Paul's green eyes; they sparkled and didn't lose contact with hers. Her intuition told her that he wasn't lying. Now she felt a bit guilty for having been so harsh. She sighed and gave in.

"I'm sorry. I don't mean to come off this way. Midterms," Claire said.

"It's cool. I get it," Paul said, putting his hands on the edge of her desk.

"So, what's really going on?" Claire asked, resting her hand on his hand in an attempt to make him forget about her harsh reaction just minutes ago. "I feel like every time I see you now you're bringing something up about your sister. Is she going to be okay?"

"Honestly … I don't know," Paul said, putting his head down. "She was just diagnosed as severely bipolar a few months ago."

"I, uhh … wow," Claire said. "I'm officially a monster. I feel bad. Anything I can do to help?"

"Nah, not at all," Paul said. "You're fine."

"And you're obviously not," Claire said. "What happened?"

"I don't know," Paul said. "Last night when I 'blew you off,' I was actually picking her up from a nightclub. Phoenix—it's a little outside of Cambridge. Apparently, she got kicked out with some guy. She said he had started a fight. I could tell she hadn't taken her meds. It was … insane. She was dressed in this ridiculous outfit—something the normal Libby would never wear, and she wasn't listening to rational thought at all." Paul sighed and rubbed the back of his neck.

Claire was taken aback by Paul's problem. Up until now, she had never really seen him as a sensitive person. She had always assumed he was that shirtless and ego-driven guy she had first met. She forgot that he could have feelings, too. It made her even more attracted to him, and she became flustered until she saw her computer screen light up with a familiar message notification.

YOU HAVE #1 NEW MESSAGE FROM {Z}.

Claire didn't want this right now. This was the worst possible timing. She tried to close the notification but accidentally clicked it open.

· *And the twins shall now wreak their havoc :-)*

Z at 4:12pm

Claire clicked in desperation to get out of the message but was met with three photo attachments that popped up. They were pictures of Kevin and a girl dancing closely together at a nightclub. She recognized the girl at once—it was Paul's sister, Libby.

"Something wrong?" Paul asked.

Claire began to click with even more desperation but her computer seemed frozen with these images stuck on the forefront. Paul came around her desk to see what she was looking at. She gave up on trying and took the next best option. With a swift maneuver, Claire reached to the side of the monitor and shut it off. Paul arrived behind her, confused about what had just happened.

"Uh, porn," Claire said. "Oh, gosh. Umm ... that sounded horrible. It was spam. But porn. Porn spam."

Paul gave her a slow nod to convey that he wasn't convinced she was okay. She wasn't. As Paul pulled up a chair next to her, Claire's mind focused on Z's message. She thought about the photos. She had never seen Kevin like that with anyone. And what was he doing at a club like that—he was underage! Her disappointment grew as she wondered why he hadn't told her about this to begin with. She knew this could be disastrous if Paul found out. Something wasn't right.

"Hey. You sure nothing is wrong?" Paul asked.

Claire looked at the dead monitor screen then back at Paul. "Yeah, I'm sure."

☙

Sam reached for the door and then walked away again. He had been repeating this move for ten minutes and was beginning to realize how stupid he must have looked. He looked at the card in the palm of his hand that had enticed him to be where he was. Doctor Eva had left a lasting impression on him. Even so, he had no courage to walk into her office with these newfound feelings. He determined that it would be better to put this meeting off until the next day—as he had done already the day before—and he started to venture back to his dorm. After a long walk, Sam finally got back to his dorms and felt unaccomplished. As he walked down the hall to his door, he noticed something that concerned him. Kevin, who was normally in good spirits, sat in front of Sam's door with his head resting on his propped-up knees. Sam looked around and then walked up to his friend.

"Don't take this the wrong way, but … you look like crap," Sam said, nudging Kevin's knee with his foot.

"Nice to see you too," Kevin said as he stood up. "Sam, something bad happened last night."

"Dude. *Shhh*. What are you doing?" Sam said as he rushed Kevin into his dorm and shut the door. "You know who is probably watching via drone satellite. If this has anything to do with the mistresses … inside talk only."

Kevin plopped on one of Sam's old chairs and leaned back as if he'd had too much to eat. He let out a groan and covered his eyes with his hands.

"Oh. Uh oh. This is bad," Sam said. "What happened?"

Kevin sighed. "Last night … I went out with this girl named Libby," he said.

"Yeah. I know her," Sam said.

"Umm, how?" Kevin sat upright and stared at Sam.

"Journalism club. Spy break-in. Long story," Sam said.

Kevin rolled his eyes and leaned back in the chair. "Yeah, well she pretty much left me for dead at Club Phoenix last night. I don't know what got into her. She was making out with another guy practically in front of me. It was crazy. I almost got into a huge fight with the guy before the bouncers threw me out. That was fun. Oh, and then I went outside the club to try to find her and figured out that she had ditched me because she was nowhere to be seen. We're meeting up in a bit to talk about it, and I hope it was all just a big misunderstanding. It couldn't possibly get any worse, right?"

"Kevin, what sign is she?" Sam asked in a serious tone.

"Can we just leave that out of this for once?" Kevin asked. "Not every girl has to be a mistress you know."

"Dude. What sign is she?" Sam asked again.

Kevin looked out the window and sighed. "She's a Gemini," he said.

Sam wasted no time opening up his Zodiac booklet, along with Kubo's notes. He enjoyed being the smart one for once. More important, this was his way of sticking to the pact they had all made.

"Okay, look. Gemini mistress," Sam said pointing to a page in his booklet.

Kevin looked on, hoping he wouldn't find anything bad. His fears were well-founded. The artwork on Kubo's page was dark: Two twin women stood back to back. Their hair stood fierce and bold. While they were clearly beautiful, they also seemed to have a furious nature to them. The image gave both Kevin and Sam chills. Sam began to read aloud the description.

> "The Gemini Mistress—a sign who lives from May 21ˢᵗ through June 21ˢᵗ.
>
> Deep intimacy cannot be matched against the Gemini mistress' charm,
>
> They are gentle in all, and most would not do any harm.
>
> But beware. For just as the Gemini mistress has a loving side,
>
> They can switch with their twin, a fate with a face of devilish eyes."

"Okay. Not too bad. Could be worse, I guess," Sam said.

"No, you don't get it, dude," Kevin said. "I don't want Libby to be a Zodiac mistress. I like her. Last night was wild, but invigorating. She brought out a fun and rambunctious side of me. I think I may try to get out of this Zodiac thing."

Sam's eye widened. "But you risk losing true love for the rest of your life. You signed the parchment."

"But what if it's all fake?" Kevin asked. "What if nothing happens at all and I end up finding love right here, right now?"

"And what if it's not?" Sam asked.

Kevin grunted in frustration at Sam.

"There's one more thing, actually. About Libby," Kevin said. "I found out last night that she's Paul's sister."

"Well that's just great. This is going to end real well," Sam said with a sarcastic tone. "Where's Claire when you need her? She would know what to do."

"No," Kevin said as he stood up and headed for the door. "Sam, Claire can't know right now. I don't want to cause any drama between her and Paul you know? Look I gotta go. I'm gonna meet up with Libby and try to fix things."

Sam didn't respond. He looked away as Kevin closed the door behind him. With no idea how to protect his friend and prevent this situation from taking a turn for the worse, Sam looked at Eva's card for relief.

☽

Kevin walked up to Libby, who was sitting on a red and black checkered wool blanket on the grass. Her eyes were locked on the night sky. It was a quiet night. Normally the Cambridge playing field would have some kind of sporting event or pep rally to spark campus spirit, but on this night, the looming Spring quarter exams left the west field empty as students packed into the library to study. Kevin took a moment to take in what she was looking at and then took a seat next to her. This was the first silence that had ever been awkward between them.

"I was starting to think you weren't going to show up," Libby said. "It probably would have been a smart idea anyway, and I would have understood."

Kevin didn't respond. He knew why he was there. He just hoped that she knew.

"You seem like you're mad," Libby said. She looked at him for the first time since he'd arrived.

Kevin sighed. "I don't know, Libby. Last night was really messed up. I mean, what the hell?" he said.

"Ugh, I know," Libby said. She sat to face Kevin. "And I feel terrible about it. It's just ... well, I kind of have some things going on with me that no one would really understand."

"So that's your excuse?" Kevin said. "You dance with some random guy after inviting me to go clubbing with you? And then you practically make out with him right in front of me. And to top it off, you watch as the same random guy nearly beats the crap out of me. Then, after all that, you leave me at the club and I have no idea where you went off to. And you can't even give me a real reason why? Ugh, you're right. Maybe it wasn't a smart idea to come here." Kevin crossed his arms across his chest.

There was another awkward silence, and Kevin waited for her to say something—anything. He wanted to be sure that he wasn't just wasting his time. Even though she happened to fit into the next part of his Zodiac quest, he wanted to see her as something more. So when the silence lasted for longer than he could stand, he began to get up.

"I have severe bipolar disorder," Libby blurted out. She watched as Kevin sat back down. "The night we were at the club ... well, I hadn't taken my meds in a couple of days. I wasn't myself. Or maybe I *was* myself. I don't know actually ... I called my brother to come to the rescue like I always do, and then I remembered you guys aren't on the best of terms. So I panicked and left with him, leaving you behind. I'm sorry, I didn't know what else to do."

Kevin took a moment to absorb everything. Her honesty helped to make up for the unpleasantness of the previous night. Her vulnerability made her craziness seem beautiful and enticing.

"So what now?" Kevin said. He inched closer to Libby.

"Now is the time when you tell me I'm a psycho and then you leave me here all alone," Libby said with her head down. She nervously flicked some grass off the blanket.

"I don't think that," Kevin said, as he put his hand under her chin and turned her head up to face him. Her skin was velvety soft and smooth—Kevin could run his fingers along it all night long.

They both smiled. The awkwardness was gone.

"You're a work of art, Kevin Deer," Libby said. The usual soft caramel color in her eyes sparkled at Kevin and she looked innocent again, just as when he'd met her that first night at the observatory.

Kevin caught himself staring intently into Libby's eyes. A bond had formed between them, forged from the most unbreakable material. He looked down as he felt her hand rest gently on his thigh. He leaned in and kissed her. She kissed him back, and a series of subtle rubs and passionate grabs ensued. They threw her wool blanket over themselves to keep their activity secret. Kevin looked into Libby's eyes. "Are you sure about this?" Kevin asked.

Libby bit her lip and pulled him in. The next passing moments under the stars were like blossoms, as the clouds seemed to move across the sky. The night hid everything but bare skin and romantic whispers. The stars witnessed love being made.

All this went on until dawn broke. On a night that was meant for a simple chat, they had slept together and become lost in serenity. As the sun danced across their eyelids, they woke up and felt closer than they ever had. Libby looked at Kevin and smiled. He smiled back at her and sighed. He reached toward her, thinking she was reaching for him, but then he realized she was just grabbing her backpack. He watched as she pulled out a bottle of water and an orange pill container. In seconds, she had taken her stabilizer. And just as quickly as Kevin had begun to feel the perfect emotion for someone, he began to feel a trace of concern. Still, he hoped that things would work out for once.

☽

Sam was up all night tossing and turning. The last few days and nights had proven to be stressful. This particular night, Sam's thoughts were on the matter of Kevin and Libby and their love. Giving up trying to force himself to sleep, he took out Kubo's Zodiac book once more to learn about what was troubling him. Sam felt an obligation to help Kevin and digested what knowledge he could to find any loopholes in the parchment Kevin had signed.

Finally, he discovered something unusual. In the back of the book, Kubo had listed a few intriguing items. The first of these items was a date, which was roughly thirteen months before they'd found the book. The second was a series of twelve Zodiac symbols, eleven of which had been crossed out. Sam wondered if this meant anything. He then noticed a third item—it looked like a code. The numbers read, "FB 06.13.82." To Sam, these numbers were a captivating puzzle. He racked his brain, trying to figure out what the abbreviation "FB" stood for. He felt it had a familiar ring. And as the bell tower went off to announce dawn, Sam's brain struck a chord of understanding.

"Faculty box. 'FB.' It's a faculty box!" Sam said.

Sam ran through the numbers once more and realized that this could be either a birthdate or a combination code. He threw Kubo's book in his bag and rushed so quickly out of his dorm that he didn't even straighten up his hair. Sam knew that in order to have a chance at examining this mystery, he would have to get into the main offices before the janitorial staff locked the building as they finished their nightly cleaning. By his watch, he had about forty minutes. He knew he would need every last one of them.

Sam surveyed the front of the Cambridge faculty building as inconspicuously as he could. It wasn't against campus policy to be in the area, so it wasn't suspicious for him to be hanging around the building. In fact, some students even worked in the building. He decided to walk in as a few janitors washed windows and buffed floors. Sam gave them a nervous smile. They ignored him and kept working. Their inattention was enough to put Sam at ease, and so he ventured to the next floor, where he had a hunch the faculty boxes were. He got on the elevator, which was just as cold as it was empty. As the elevator carried him to his floor, the seconds crept by with mind-numbing slowness. He decided to distract himself from his anxiety by reciting the code he'd found in Kubo's book.

"FB 06.13.82. FB 06.13.82. FB 06.13.82," Sam whispered, tapping his foot on the floor.

Sam's repetitive chant was interrupted by a quick ring. The elevator has stopped on the second floor. Cautiously, Sam got off the elevator and surveyed the floor. It was a bit of an eerie scene. No one had made it into the office yet, so the floor was dimly lit with a few flickering hallway lights. The silence was as still as Sam was trying to be. He did his best to swallow his fear as he began to walk toward the school faculty resource center. If there were any lockers or boxes, he figured this would be the best place to look.

"This is definitely creepy," Sam muttered.

Sam walked to the main door and realized it was an electric keypad lock that needed badge access. He stood for a couple of minutes, thinking about what to do. He couldn't get in. He almost gave up and turned away, but then the doorknob began to turn. Sam's fear heightened. He ducked to the side in the dark and tried to figure out an excuse should he be caught. A light peered through the hallway and then shut off. A janitor, with loud music blasting through his headphones, continued pushing his cleaning cart, paying no attention to Sam.

Sam acted fast and jumped into the room as the door slowly shut behind him. Once the coast was clear, he flipped on the light switch.

The office was a dignified headquarters of plush leather seats and administrative tools. To his left, he noticed a door with a window in it. He looked through and saw a row of what looked like safety deposit boxes. He opened the door and scanned each one to see if they matched the numbers that were now stuck in his head. None of them were numbered. Instead, he found they were labeled with the names of the professors in alphabetical order. He went down the rows and soon found Kubo's name listed. He recited the numbers again.

"FB 06.13.82," Sam said.

He realized it was a combination and scrambled it in. The lock clicked into place and the box opened up—and Sam was dumbfounded. Inside the box was a single envelope. He picked it up and looked around. He knew his time was running out. As he proceeded out the door, he began to feel as though someone had been watching him. He looked around after he thought he heard some shuffling. He didn't want to find out who it might be, so he rushed to the elevator and pushed the button, praying silently for the doors to close faster. Once the elevator doors shut, Sam breathed a sigh of relief. This relief was short-lived, however—when he looked at his phone to get the time, he saw a text message from Z, confirming his fear that a stalker was on his trail.

From 617-682-7897 at 6:48 am: Tsk, tsk, tsk. You shouldn't stick your nose into things that don't concern you. Time for havoc to begin. —Z

Sam held his phone tight as he exited the elevator. The janitors looked at him for a second and then continued their work. Z could have been any one of them. Sam didn't have the courage or curiosity to find out and ran as fast as he could to Kevin's dorm.

☙

Kevin looked at his phone once more. It was his seventh text to Libby over the last two days and there was no answer. He sighed and wondered if she'd lost her feelings for him after their experience in the campus field.

Suddenly he was startled out of his gloom by the sound of someone pounding on his door and calling his name. He opened the door to see Sam who looked frantic. He let Sam in and watched as he panted for oxygen.

"Have. Something. Important. To show. You," Sam gasped.

Kevin grabbed the envelope that Sam was holding out. It was a simple, ordinary envelope. The back was inscribed, "To my darling." Kevin looked at it and then looked at Sam.

"I found it in Kubo's faculty box," Sam explained. Kevin shook his head as he opened up the envelope. He wondered what trouble his friend had gotten into now.

Inside the envelope were two handwritten letters. The first, in the same handwriting as the writing on the outside of the envelope, was an anonymous note.

To my darling,
Words can't describe how sorry I am. It
is my deepest desire for us to be together,
but as you know that would be impossible.
Even now, I feel guilty for writing this. Maybe
one day we will be able to be together. But
right now that is something that I can't give
you. I hope you find happiness. You are the
sweetest man I know. You deserve all of
that and more.
—Forever, your dearest

He then read the second letter.

To my friends and my family, who meant the
world to me,
I am sorry I must leave you all this way.
I was not strong enough. I'm asking you to
be stronger than I was. And to my dearest,
as my heart continues to suffer, I pray you
see this goodbye as my last act of love for
you. I wish you all well.
With the deepest love,
James

Kevin felt a clenching sensation in his chest when he realized how this letter related to the first letter. He looked back
up at Sam. They both were speechless. They had both read
Professor Kubo's suicide note.

"Do you think that maybe Kubo's dearest is Z?" Sam asked.

Before Kevin could answer, he was interrupted by another onslaught of knocks at his door. Sam panicked.

"That's it man. We're officially dead now," Sam said.

"Would you shut up," Kevin said.

Kevin took his time opening the door. Looking through the crack, he saw Claire and Paul there standing together. Both appeared to be in a tense mood as Claire led the way in, pushing Kevin's door open. Sam scowled at Paul, who shut the door in a rough fashion.

"Why is he here?" Sam said.

"Stop. Just stop. Okay," Claire said, holding her hands in front of Paul. She turned and looked at Kevin. "Kevin, it's Libby."

"I know about the club," Paul said, pointing in Kevin's face. "I don't know what you're trying to pull you little piece of—"

"Hey. Stop. Enough of this," Claire said to Paul. "We're not going to find her by getting upset. Besides, Kevin would *never* intentionally harm anyone."

Paul let out a sigh and backed away from Kevin. Kevin, whose morning had now transformed into an odd stew of complex emotions, looked at Claire and everyone else with a frightening realization.

"Where is she?" Kevin said.

Claire signaled Paul, who pulled out his phone with his head hanging low, his hands shaking with anger and worry. He clicked on a series of buttons and handed the phone to Kevin.

On the screen was a text. It was a simple message, but a dark one. Libby had sent a farewell message to Paul and a photo of a message she'd received from Z. Every word in Z's message struck keys of sabotage.

> From 617-682-7897 at 11:41 pm: Kevin only slept with you to fulfill a quest. He didn't truly care about you. Now you can share the same fate as Laura and Gracie. Checkmate Gemini. Checkmate. —Z

Kevin put the phone down and saw the concern in everyone's eyes. He presumed it mirrored his own. Claire seemed especially upset. He couldn't imagine how betrayed she felt after realizing she had been kept in the dark about Libby and Kevin's budding romance. He wondered if this had messed things up for her and Paul.

"When did you see her last?" Claire asked.

"It was the other night. We spent it out on the fields. She took some pills when she woke up. I thought she was okay."

"You knew about her problem and still had the nerve to screw her over like this!" Paul said. He was getting worked up again and his face was turning red.

"Paul. Stop. We won't find her if we act like this," Claire said. "We should start looking. I'll go with Kevin to look around campus, and Sam you go with Paul to look around town."

"Why do I have—" Sam started to say.

"I don't want to hear it!" Claire said. "We're all in this together. We need to find her. Especially since she's not well."

☙

"Watch where you're going! Geez," Sam said to a car that nearly ran into him and Paul as they crossed the street.

Sam rarely ventured into the city. He didn't like the business of it all—it annoyed him. And now that he was with Paul, the experience proved to be that much more frustrating. He looked at Paul, who was as quiet as a rock.

"What a day, right?" Sam said.

Paul grunted and Sam decided to try again. "Boy, I bet Claire and Kevin are having just as much luck as us—"

"God, would you shut the hell up already!" Paul yelled. "I'm not here to make friends with you. I'm here to find my sister. Stop trying to make this some sort of bonding trip. We're not buddies. I could care less about you or your good-for-nothing friend Deer."

Sam paused. "What about Claire?" he asked.

Paul scoffed. "What about her?" he said. "Look. You know the game. Popular guy. Cute girl. It is what it is."

Sam was infuriated. How could he talk about someone like Claire in that way? All Sam could think about was how much of a jerk Paul was. But then again, maybe he was a jerk himself for not standing up for Claire.

"Here it is," Paul said. "Club Phoenix."

Sam and Paul looked up to see a tacky neon sign hanging over a bouncer with a frown on his face and his arms folded tightly over his chest. The noise coming from the club made it clear why it was so popular. Every beat invited you in. Sam and Paul ignored the urge and walked to the bouncer, whose scowl grew even more intense.

"Excuse me. But have you seen this girl?" Sam asked, holding his phone out to show him a photo of Libby.

"Maybe. What's in it for me?" said the bouncer.

Sam and Paul looked at each other and dug through their pockets. They pulled together a few crumpled bills. They knew it wouldn't be enough to convince the bouncer to give them what they needed, and looked up to see him indeed losing interest in their efforts.

"I have about six bucks," Sam said.

"That's better than my three," Paul said.

"We have nine dollars," Paul said and shoved the crumpled bills under the bouncer's nose.

The bouncer's silence told them enough. Thinking about what to do next, Sam's attention drifted to Paul's watch. Paul noticed him staring at it.

"Seriously?" Paul said, gripping the watch tightly to his wrist.

"Do you want to find Libby or not?" Sam said.

Paul let out a sigh as he undid his gold watch. The bouncer's forehead unwrinkled; he was paying attention now. Sam watched as Paul regretfully handed his watch over.

"Yeah. I recognize her," the bouncer said. "She was here the other day with some guy. Caused some drama and there was a fight. She comes here a lot though. She's on the VIP list."

"Is she inside right now?" Paul said.

"Nope. I remember everyone who walks in and walks out. She's not inside, sorry," the bouncer said.

Sam shrugged his shoulders as Paul frowned at him.

"Now what, genius?" Paul asked as he turned his back to the bouncer to confront Sam.

"I guess we're out of luck," Sam shrugged.

"Wait," the bouncer said. "She's not inside, but she did stop by here. I couldn't let her in after the incident the other night."

Paul grew tense. "Where is she?" he said.

"She headed that way," the bouncer threw his hand in one direction. "She mentioned something about some observatory or something like that. Yeah." He then went back to tending to his clipboard, signaling to the boys that he had given them all the info he felt appropriate for his "pay."

Sam and Paul looked in the direction he pointed.

☽

"So are you going to ignore me the whole time?" Claire asked.

Kevin tried to look as interested as he could in the surrounding campus fields. It was his way of keeping his mind off things. He didn't want to think of anything else except finding Libby.

"Kevin—" Claire said as she paused in her tracks.

Kevin turned to see that Claire had folded her arms and was frowning. Everything leading up until now made way for this moment. It was inevitable. He sighed.

"You think it's okay to bring my mortal enemy by my dorm room?" Kevin said.

"He may be your mortal enemy, but he's the guy I'm currently dating who happens to be the brother of the girl you're apparently involved with," Claire said.

"Great choice. You sure know how to pick them," Kevin said.

"What's that supposed to mean?" Claire said.

"Forget it," Kevin said.

"No," Claire said. "What's that supposed to mean, huh?"

Claire walked up to Kevin and pushed him. Kevin, who had seen this side of Claire once before, knew this was her way of expressing extreme passion. She pushed him again, a bit harder this time.

"What's that supposed to mean, huh?" Claire repeated.

And as she landed a punch in Kevin's chest, he couldn't help but see what her eyes really meant. He let her have her way until she became exhausted. She looked up with a guilty look and gave him one last shove.

"You don't get to do that," Claire said. Her eyes started to mist. "You don't get to criticize."

"I'm not trying to criticize," Kevin said. "I'm sorry."

"Why didn't you tell me about the club? Or Libby's condition?" Claire asked. "We used to tell each other everything. Talk about anything."

"I know," Kevin said. He put his head down.

Claire saw she had made her point. It was her way of keeping what she held dear. It was her way of showing she cared.

"Look, just promise me," Claire said. "*No* more secrets."

"Deal," Kevin said.

"Good. Because next time I may aim for your face," Claire said.

She gave him one final, playful shove and Kevin let out a faint laugh. They hugged, and if the hug had been held for just a slight second longer, there probably would have been a spark. But it didn't happen. Instead, they were interrupted by a buzz from Kevin's cell phone in his front pocket. Claire tucked her hair behind her ears, feeling awkward at the moment they had just shared.

Kevin couldn't pay attention to any of that. He had to check his phone. It might be Libby, letting him know she was okay, or maybe it was Sam and Paul confirming that they had found her safe.

But it wasn't either of those. Kevin looked at Claire after he checked his phone. She knew that look all too well.

"Let me see," Claire said, grabbing Kevin's phone.

> *From 617-682-7897 at 8:19 pm: I hear you're looking for someone. Might I suggest looking from a distance? Do hurry. The clock is ticking. ;-) —Z*

"You thinking what I'm thinking? Kevin asked.

"The observatory," Claire said. "Text Sam and Paul."

Kevin nodded. In a split second they were off and running. In the back of both of their minds, one question stood out more than anything. What did Z mean by "Clock is ticking?"

Kevin and Claire rushed up the final flight of stairs and landed at the observatory deck, where the fresh air cooled them down. They were relieved to see Sam and Paul already standing there, but they noticed Libby was nowhere in sight.

Kevin was out of breath. It seemed as though the only place to look was over the balcony. The sun had set now—and Kevin was glad because the darkness could hide his concern. Sam came up to him and put a hand on his shoulder. Behind them they could hear Claire and Paul bickering.

"I think it's time we get the police involved, buddy," Sam said. "Z's not gonna let us win."

Kevin looked back at Sam, Paul, and Claire. This was all his fault. He didn't dare try to make an excuse. But he remained hopeful and optimistic—they could solve this—and he would lead them. But then the meaning of Z's words came over him like a rush of new air. Kevin stumbled as he looked around. There it was. A simple brass telescope connected to a fixture on the balcony. Kevin rushed over to it as everyone looked at him with confusion.

"This is it," Kevin shouted to the group as he pointed at the telescope.

"What gives?" Paul muttered.

"From a distance," Kevin said, repeating the words from Z's latest clue. "From a distance. We've got to be able to see her through here. Look how it was set up—just for us."

Kevin looked through the clear lens of the telescope, taking care not to move it from its original position. It lined up perfectly in the direction of the bell tower. More precisely, it lined up perfectly with the opening terrace right above the clock. There stood Libby—feeble and alone. Kevin panicked when he noticed that she was standing on the edge. She was peering down.

"Oh no," Kevin said. "No. No. No." He put his hands up to his head and shook his head back and forth.

"What?" Claire asked.

Kevin had no time to answer. He rushed off. Claire looked through the telescope and paused.

"Guys," Claire said. "We need to get over to the bell tower. Quick."

Everyone sprinted closely behind Kevin. He led the pack with heroism fueled by both love and hate: His love for Libby drove his speed, and his hatred of the situation supported his endurance. He looked up as he neared the bell tower.

"Libby!" Kevin yelled. "What are you doing? This is dangerous. I'm coming up!"

"No!" Libby said. "Don't you dare. This is all your fault. It's your fault that I got the messages."

"Paul," Claire said, resting her hand on Paul's arm, gently holding him back. "Why don't you let us distract her and you can go up there when she won't notice. Then you can grab her."

Paul nodded. He looked at Kevin and Sam, who both silently agreed with Claire's game plan.

"Libby," Kevin said, looking back up at the first girl he had been intimate with since Susan.

Libby looked down at him. The light of the moon allowed Kevin to see the tears streaming down Libby's cheeks. It was the first time Libby had looked directly at anybody. Kevin hoped this meant she would accept his help.

"Please. Don't do this," Kevin said. "Let me come up there and talk to you. Just us."

"How do I know you won't hurt me?" Libby said in between her sobs. "The messages. Were they true? How could you do this to me, Kevin? We made *love*. I let you be my first!"

Kevin paused. He could feel the stares. He looked back to see Claire standing with folded arms and Sam grinning nervously.

"Libby," Kevin said. " I promise. I never meant to hurt you. Just come down so we can talk about this."

"No!" Libby yelled. "You're lying! You're a liar Kevin Deer! And I loved you. *I. Loved. You.*"

Libby started slapping her face. Her face grew redder with every slap. Sam looked at Kevin.

"This isn't good," Sam said. "Kevin, you should get up to the top of the tower with Paul. She's going to slap herself right off the ledge. I think Claire and I can keep distracting her, right Claire?" Sam looked to Claire for reassurance.

Claire huffed. "Fine. Yes, Kevin, go."

Claire looked up at Libby. "Libby ... my word may not mean much, but just listen to me. Kevin—he's not like other guys. He truly cares about you. Just like he cares about me and Sam and ... well, everybody he meets."

Libby stopped slapping herself and looked down at Claire. "Really?" she asked, sniffling.

Kevin raced up the bell tower steps and saw Paul slowly sneaking toward Libby as quietly as he could. Libby suddenly noticed everyone's silence down below. She jerked around as she guessed they were watching someone behind her and almost lost her balance, which caused Paul to lunge forward.

"No!" Libby screamed, her face red and swollen. "You're not going to stop me. I've already made my choice."

"Libby ... please," Paul said, tearing up. He reached out his hand.

Libby gave it no second thought. She hovered her right foot off the ledge and leaned backward as Paul rushed toward her. She heard a gasp down below as Claire and Sam looked on in disbelief. She closed her eyes and quietly counted to herself. *1 ... 2 ... 3 ...*

Kevin had rushed up right behind Paul and positioned himself behind a pillar, but as soon as Libby closed her eyes, he took action. He had to. His heart moved him forward without hesitation. And with every ounce of athleticism he possessed, he leaped forward on Libby's count of 3 and grabbed her right arm just in time. She slammed against the side of the bell tower as Kevin clung to her arm with as much strength as he could muster. "LET GO OF ME!" she screamed and tried to wriggle out of Kevin's grip.

Kevin could hear Sam mutter, "Oh. My. God" and figured Claire was in a silent panic. Then he saw another hand grab onto Libby's arm. It was Paul, pulling Libby back up over the bell tower ledge.

Kevin's arm was bleeding, as it had scraped against the wall of the bell tower while he held onto Libby. Libby's face had been cut up, her arm was bent, and bruises would surely start to form by the next day.

Kevin and Paul grabbed Libby in a tight group hug while she sobbed uncontrollably. Claire and Sam were in the bell tower now too. Claire rubbed Paul's back while Sam got on the phone with the campus emergency hotline.

Kevin's heroics had paid off. Libby was alive.

ॐ

Medics arrived after the group had waited in silence for a while. No one felt they needed to speak. They were just happy to be okay, and even more relieved to see the medics pull up. They escorted Libby, whose arm appeared to be broken, to the truck. Sam looked over at Kevin with pride. Claire smiled at Kevin; she couldn't help but wonder if he would do the same for her. As for Paul, he was still on the fence about Kevin. His look said it all.

"Well, I guess I owe you some thanks," Paul said. "So … thanks."

Kevin looked at him, and nodded, figuring that was better than no recognition at all. He watched Libby being strapped into the back of the ambulance. He knew he needed to say goodbye. Everyone else looked on as he did. It was a simple moment, one that didn't need much explaining. Kevin looked at Libby and she looked at him. The smile they exchanged showed they both knew this would be the end of their romance. And even though he wanted to speak, he felt more inclined to keep his words to himself. He waved instead. It was his way of saying that he loved her too. Paul climbed into the back of the ambulance to go with her and gave Kevin a nod. and just as quickly as Libby had fallen into Kevin's arms, she was gone.

"She's going to be fine," Claire said, rubbing Kevin's back in reassurance.

"I hope so," Kevin said.

Sam walked up and took in a deep breath. He felt a sense of relief.

"So … I guess this means you've officially made it through three Zodiac signs, right?" Sam said. "Who would have thought this was how our junior year would end. You sure all this is worth it, man?"

Kevin thought about it. Being sure was far from his mind. After everything with Libby, Kevin felt as though another heartbreak would be too much. But just as he was about to answer Sam's question with a firm no, a spark appeared within him. It was the same spark that started this journey—the one that gave him hope for love's bountiful harvest.

"Yeah. I'm sure," Kevin said firmly.

That noble answer was followed by dings and vibrations. Kevin, Claire, and Sam all looked at each other and then at their phones. They had all received the same message from the same person.

> From 617-682-7897 at 11:50 pm: You will not win the war. Young love can only go so far. Hahahaha. —Z

Despite Z's cryptic message, everyone felt a bit of relief— Z had just admitted that they had won something.

As they walked back to their dorms, Kevin felt even closer to his goal of true love. Claire thought about the hug Kevin had given her earlier and was convinced that this was bringing them closer together. Sam thought about Claire and Paul.

"I just realized something," Sam said, and he stopped in his tracks.

Kevin and Claire stopped alongside him and listened with anticipation. It seemed as though Sam had reached some kind of deep conclusion. And he had.

"I think I know why Kubo committed suicide," Sam said. "I think he failed the quest for the twelve mistresses."

CHAPTER V

—THE CANCER WHO CRIED CHEAT—

Cancer: June 21st—July 23rd

The Cancer, an emotional water sign, is often seen as nurturing, but her extreme sensitivity can mislead her suitors. There are none greater in sensitivity than the Cancer Mistress—they are emotional and harmonious and dedicated to finding the right "fix" to any problem. However, that same caring nature renders the Cancer weak when it comes time to confront a painful or difficult situation. While Kevin and his friends have overcome great adversity on this journey of love, they may soon realize that not every mistress is in the form of an obvious lover.

☽

Kevin stared at the pen as Dean Keller tapped it rhythmically on his oak desk. The dean's desk made a unique fortress.

A moat of neat papers separated them. Their surroundings, while suited well in school spirit, created a condescending tone. Keller looked at Kevin with a mixture of concern and frustration. He had soft eyes but a hard face—one that had been shaped by years of sleepless nights.

"You must excuse the random meeting, Mr. Deer. But I hope you can see why I'm expressing my concern," said Keller. "You and your friends are somehow connected to quite the commotion here at Cambridge."

Kevin knew this was true. In just three months he had witnessed a girl attempt to murder a professor with a golf cart, another girl ruin Spring Fling with a twisted video that caused students to break into a fight, and now a girl had attempted suicide on the bell tower not too long after she'd lost her virginity to him. It was enough drama to make anybody's head spin. Even so, his heart had never burned brighter. He was determined to find true love.

"In light of all that's happened, might I suggest you see a school counselor," Keller said, as he put his pen down and began to tap his fingers on his desk.

"Well, I don't really feel as though I need one, sir. I feel fine," Kevin said.

Keller's frown stiffened. "Mr. Deer. I should be more clear," he said as he cleared his throat. "I'm not suggesting. I'm telling. Consider this an act of mercy. The board is all over me about your connection to these strange events. They are suggesting suspension. I can persuade them to move away from that idea if you agree to attend school counseling. Do I make myself clear?"

Kevin put his head down. Keller looked at him and could sense why. They both did their best to keep quiet about their true intentions.

"You won't be alone," Keller said. "Your two friends will also join you. In separate sessions of course. I've already spoken to them and they understand. I trust you will make the best decision."

Keller handed Kevin a pamphlet with a business card attached to it.

"Eva Keller?" Kevin asked confused.

"Oh, yes. My wife," Keller said. "She's a counselor here with a great deal of experience. You'll be in good hands with her."

Kevin stood up and shoved all of the information into his pants pocket. Keller stood to see Kevin out the door. Neither of them was thrilled to shake hands, but the tension eased as they knew the meeting was finally coming to an end.

"Mr. Deer," Keller said. "I understand you've been through a lot recently. You'll do the right thing, won't you?"

"Yes, sir," Kevin said.

Keller nodded and waved Kevin away. Kevin was relieved that it wasn't as bad as it could have been. He exited Keller's office and let out a sigh; he hoped that everything would be worth all of this.

☙

Claire walked into the counseling offices earlier than her scheduled appointment time. She felt she needed to. She was actually looking forward to her counseling session. Between the drama with her new boyfriend Paul, Cambridge spring semester finals, and the increasing drama of the Zodiac journey, she was losing sleep and had forgotten about most everything else in her life. She was feeling lost and confused, and she hadn't felt safe in quite some time.

She took a look around and realized that she didn't have to check in at the front desk. The admin who sat the front desk, a girl about Claire's age, was too busy flirting with a young man showing off his new watch to her. Claire chose to ignore the annoying giggles and take in the more calming effect of the office. In doing so, she realized there was a soothing kind of zen that enveloped everything. Bamboo and jade souvenirs made up most of the decor. A small fountain babbled in the background. It was a peaceful scene, and that peace was reinforced by walls covered in framed psychology certifications and positive quotes. And yet, Claire still couldn't bring herself to have any faith in this place. She was disheveled—which was the first thing Eva noticed after she waved Claire into her private room.

"Long day, my darling?" Eva said after she closed her door and sat down in front of Claire.

Claire started fixing herself up; she smoothed her hair down and wiped underneath her eyes, hoping to wipe away any smudges of mascara. She noticed how well Eva was dressed and began to adjust her own clothes even more.

"So it has been?" Eva asked. "A long day?"

"Well, yeah, I guess it has," Claire said as she tried to smooth out the wrinkles on her khaki uniform skirt. She crossed her feet at her ankles to try to hide the dirt on the edges of her socks. "I'm sure it could be for anyone, though."

Eva adjusted her designer brand glasses as if she needed to better see into Claire. Claire felt awkward. The silence created a stale ambiance.

"Well, I mean … yes. It's been a long day," Claire said and looked to Eva for her approval.

Claire felt like Eva was staring right into her brain. This time Eva followed up the look with a few notes in her journal. To Claire, each scribble screamed judgment.

"Claire," Eva said setting her pen down. "You're not in trouble. There's no need to be nervous. I'm on your side."

Claire relaxed a little bit into her chair and uncrossed her feet. Her gut was sensing some kind of weird vibe, but she ignored it—she knew she could use some relief from everything.

"Now then," Eva said, picking her pen back up, "why don't we start with school. How's that going?"

"It's going okay," Claire said, picking at a thread on the sleeve of her uniform sweater.

"And friends, family?" Eva asked.

Claire instantly thought of Kevin. The tug of war in her heart had resurfaced. She refused to let anyone know about that but herself, however, so she ignored the question as best as she could.

"They're fine," Claire said.

Eva paused again. "How about we dig a little deeper for this first time around," she said. "I feel like you have something pressing on your mind. You've been through a lot recently, haven't you?"

If you only knew. Claire thought to herself.

"Come now, Claire," Eva said. "You couldn't possibly expect me to believe that you're not affected somehow by all of the drama you're connected to. What about your new boyfriend? How does he feel about it?"

Claire froze and gazed back at Eva in surprise. *How did she know about the new relationship?* she thought.

"There's the attention I was hoping for," Eva said as she pointed her pen at Claire. She grinned.

"How did you know?" Claire asked.

"Sweet child," Eva said. "I'm a forty-year-old woman who's been around the block more than you would think. I know a thing or two about young love."

Claire couldn't respond. *Young love,* she thought.

This was all adding up too strangely for Claire. *Why was Eva pressing her so hard to talk? Aren't therapists supposed to just let you decide how much you want to share?* Claire thought about it and started to feel a little skeptical again. She wouldn't add Eva to the list of suspects just yet but she wouldn't let her guard down in front of her, just in case she was Z.

"So, the new boyfriend?" Eva repeated. "How is that going? He doesn't mind how you are?"

Claire took a moment to snap out of her new discovery. "How I am?" she asked.

"I'm sorry. That came off wrong," Eva said. "I mean, I'm assuming he doesn't have a problem with the way you dress or keep yourself?" Eva raised her eyebrows at Claire and scanned her outfit and unstyled hair one more time.

Before Claire could respond with a snippy remark of her own, she found herself thinking about her current relationship struggles, Kevin, and her luck in general when it came to finding love. Her stomach twisted with stress. It was enough to make her question who she was. She looked down at her old sneakers, crunched her toes in them, and tightly crossed her feet again at her ankles to try to hide her tattered, stained shoes.

"Not all guys care that much about appearances. Some guys like girls for their personalities." Claire retorted. Then she backed down and asked, "Well…that's what I hope anyways. Not all guys are total jerks…right?

"Claire, darling," Eva said as she leaned into Claire. "They all are."

☙

Sam was more upbeat than normal. He walked into the building labeled "General Hall," and felt like a general. It was time for him to finally face his crush on Eva. He thought about their first encounter at the comet viewing party at the observatory, and wondered if her voice was still the same. And while this crush was a force to be reckoned with, there was another, equally strong crush to deal with—he was still very much in love with Claire. It so happened that he ran into Claire as she walked out of her counseling session with Ava. She had her head down.

"Hey! How did it go?" Sam asked.

Claire looked up with frustration in her face. Her forehead was creased with wrinkles, and her eyes were dull. It looked like she had the world on her mind. "Just leave me alone, will you," she said, pushing Sam aside.

Sam jumped back as if trying to avoid a bite from a vicious animal. Although he had seen Claire upset before, this was different. He watched as she jogged off, and shrugged his shoulders, deciding to write the matter off as something that involved hormones and a lack of sleep. Before he could think any further, Eva opened the door.

"Hi, Sam," Eva cooed. "All ready when you are."

Sam quickly forgot about Claire's outburst. He felt as though he were floating to the door, dropping from a cloud and plopping onto the couch inside the room. He was thrilled, but also nervous. Eva bent over to pick up her clipboard, and little droplets of sweat began to form on Sam's brow. As any young man would, his eyes focused on everything she revealed. Her tightly fitting dress and heels just enhanced her aura. She was stunning and confident. She was thin like a dancer, but her dress hugged her hips and gave her an hourglass shape. She was graceful on her heels—she swayed as she walked over to the chair in front of Sam and carefully crossed one leg over the other. As she sat with her legs crossed, she revealed a sneak peek of a satin slip with lace trim underneath her dress. To Sam, she was breathtaking, and he couldn't take his eyes off of her.

"My darling Sam. How are you?" Eva asked. Just like at the comet viewing party, she ran her gold ring–adorned fingers through her hair and shook her voluminous waves out to one side of her head.

Sam cleared his throat. "*Ahem* … er … I'm good." Sam blinked hard and shook his head as if to force his eyes off of her body.

"I'm glad you are here. You finally got tired of waiting by the door?" Eva asked, smiling.

Sam took a deep breath and wiped the sweat from his forehead. He had thought he was being sneaky during his previous visits; he'd never meant to let on that he was there. She must have seen him at some point. His cheeks flushed and gave his secret away. But Eva complimented Sam's actions with a wink and a mischievous smile. It was enough to leave Sam helpless as if he had melted into the couch.

"So," Eva said, "you and your friends have been quite the busy little bees. You're lucky you haven't been suspended from all of this commotion."

"Yeah," Sam said sheepishly. He put his head down. He didn't want his new love interest to regard him as the cause of the commotion.

"Hey, Sam," Eva whispered as she leaned in close to Sam. "It's okay with me. No judgment here. I think everyone should have a little adventure in their life."

Sam perked up. "Really?" he asked.

"Oh yeah. I *love* adventure," Eva said. She paused, and her mood became a bit somber. "I wish my husband were more adventurous at times." She sighed as she sat back in her chair.

Sam sat up tall on the couch. This was his second time hearing her complain about her husband. Perhaps Sam could be the adventurous guy that her husband wasn't.

"I love adventure too," Sam said. "In fact, I live for it."

Eva smiled and let out a schoolgirl giggle. "Oh, Sam," she said. "You are just too cute. What am I going to do with you, darling? How about we get started, okay?"

Sam nodded his head in agreement. They spent time talking about his classes, his parents and life at home, and how he became friends with Claire and Sam. The session was going well. Eva tried to be a little more relatable to Sam and talk about her own parents, but his mind sent him elsewhere. All he could think about was Eva's tight dress, her flirty lips, her seductive eyes. She was speaking, and he did his best to keep up with the occasional head nod, but he was lost.

"Sam?" Eva asked. "Sam? Hello?"

Sam's daydream broke. The clock next to him let off a soft alarm. His session had apparently timed out before he even knew it. He looked at Eva to see a confused face.

"You were kind of lost at the end there," Eva said.

"Yeah," Sam said. "Sorry."

Eva smiled and stood up from her seat. Her womanhood showed her exquisite definition. This made Sam all the more crazed as she sat down next to him.

"My darling, Sam," Eva said as she brushed the side of Sam's face with the tips of her soft fingers. "There's something troubling me. I feel like you may know just how to help me."

Sam looked up at Eva. Her gentle eyes showed no sign of treachery. She appeared genuine. For Sam, who had never been this close to a woman before in this manner, the experience proved to be overpowering. He could only function in two ways—he could say yes and nod in agreement. He proceeded to do both.

"You see, Sam," Eva said, as she clasped his hands in hers. "There's this rumor going around. About Professor Kubo."

Once she mentioned that name, Sam snapped back into reality and had his wits about him. She had his full attention.

"There's this thing …" Eva said taking a slight pause. "It's silly, really. I shouldn't have mentioned it. It's probably a bit *too* adventurous."

"No. No," Sam said as he turned his body to face her. "You can tell me. It's like I said before. I'm all about adventure."

Eva looked at him with a profound stare. "Can I trust you Sam?" she asked.

Sam nodded eagerly. He wanted this—to be the man she depended on.

"It's about a book that Kubo had," Eva said. "A book about finding true love."

☙

Kevin didn't know what to expect. He glanced around the office walls, which were covered in awards and bamboo plants. He turned to see Eva, who was arriving late to their meeting. As she walked into the office, she was gathering herself together. She pulled at her dress to smooth it down her body and gave her hair a quick brushing with her fingers. The somber look on her face made him question, yet again, why he had to be there.

"I'm so sorry," Eva said as she hung her coat up on a rack behind the door. "I had a client off campus."

Eva seemed to Kevin like a fragile person. Her eyelashes were fighting to contain her tears. She appeared embarrassed and sighed deeply.

"Boy, I'm just making a great first impression, aren't I?" Eva said. She turned her back to Kevin so he could not see her take a moment to wipe her eyes and take a deep breath in an attempt to become unflustered. She turned back around and sat in the chair across from Kevin. "Forgive me. It's been a rough afternoon."

"It's all right," Kevin said. "Are you okay? You seem ... upset?"

Eva laughed. "Upset isn't even the half of it," she said. "You go through all this trouble to wear his favorite outfit, just for him to barely notice, and on top of that he shows up thirty minutes late despite ..."

Kevin was a bit taken aback, and Eva noticed. He wondered if he were the one meant to provide the counseling session. There was a pause, a combination of awkward surprise and uncomfortable curiosity. During the pause, they made an unspoken mutual decision not to judge what had just happened. Neither of them felt obligated to hold onto the awkwardness for much longer.

"So, Kevin," Eva said, changing the topic. "It seems you've been making quite the commotion here at Cambridge?"

"It's bad, isn't it?" Kevin asked.

"Well, maybe not bad," Eva said. "But definitely serious. How would you say your junior year has been for you?"

Kevin took a second to think about everything that had happened. Stories of his journey nestled at the tip of his tongue. It was like word vomit, and he just wanted to spit it out. He wanted to dive into it all, especially Susan and the heartbreak he still suffered from her rejection. While every neuron jolted inside of him and urged him to divulge the truth, he couldn't. He felt too strongly his duty to keep the pact he'd made with Sam and Claire to keep the legend of the twelve mistresses sacred.

In that instant, Kevin's thoughts were suddenly interrupted by a series of sobs. Eva bent over with her hands in her face. The sight was as alarming as it was sorrowful.

"I can't anymore. I just can't," Eva said in between her sobs. She looked back up at Kevin with her makeup drizzled down her face like wet paint. "But here I am. Crying. In front of a stranger." She threw her hands in the air and continued to cry. "You have a kind face. Can I trust you, Kevin?"

Kevin had a choice to make: he could either ignore the extended hand of trust or he could embrace it. He chose the latter—after all, she had complimented him by saying his face was kind. And it was. Kevin truly felt bad for her.

"Is it something I said?" Kevin asked, knowing full well that wasn't it. He had only spoken but a few words, but he wasn't sure what else to ask her.

"Oh god, no," Eva said, as she wiped her face and smudged her makeup across her cheeks. "It certainly isn't you, Kevin. Your face is too kind for that. It's … well, it's my husband."

Alarms went off silently in Kevin's head. This was certainly territory he did not want to cross, but now he felt obligated to.

Eva continued by blowing her nose into a floral embroidered handkerchief she'd pulled out of her small clutch purse. "You see, my husband and I have been having trouble in our marriage for quite some time now. Today is my birthday, and we were supposed to have a nice lunch together."

Now the alarms reached an all-time high for Kevin. They were loud enough that he wondered if Eva could hear them. Worst of all, the alarms were *about* her: it was her birthday, and this meant that Eva was a Cancer—his next phase of the Zodiac journey. Fate had brought him together again with his next Zodiac sign. *But she isn't my age,* he thought. *She's a school counselor and way too old for me…oh, and married!*

We can't fall in love. He snapped out of his thoughts as Eva kept talking.

"He does it all the time," Eva said in a whiny, high pitched voice. "He rambles on and on about how much he loves me, and how he'll do better next time. And I keep giving in. I'm afraid to throw away all the time I've invested, you know? But I can't anymore. This isn't love. No. I felt what real love is like. Once before."

Eva ended her monologue by looking away toward the wall. She clasped her hands together and rested them in her lap. The emotion that she had let loose, given his discovery of her birth date, gave Kevin a sinking feeling in his gut. That feeling alone was enough to keep him quiet, and his thoughts flowed wildly, like a game of ping pong in his brain.

"Do you believe in love, Kevin?" Eva asked as she continued to stare at the wall.

"I'm not sure what you mean," Kevin said. "I mean I'd like to believe in it—"

"No, Kevin. Do you *believe* in it?" Eva said and then turned to look at him. "Do you believe in a love that fills you with everything you need, want, and desire? Unadulterated love. You believe in that?"

Kevin paused. He looked down as thoughts of Susan ran rampant. He looked back at Eva.

"Yes, I do," Kevin said.

Eva smiled. "There's something about you, Kevin," she said, as she grabbed her clipboard and sniffled one last time. "I think this will be good for us. Now then. Shall we begin your session?"

֍

Kevin noticed a friendlier atmosphere this time in Dean Keller's office. The usual uptight energy was replaced with smiles and offerings of water and peppermints. It was odd for Kevin to see the dean in this spirit. Perhaps this was a new fresh start. The seat he offered was the same chair as before, yet this time his enthusiasm made it seem new. Kevin sat and wondered what was happening.

"You seem so different now, Kevin. And only after one session with Eva?" Keller said.

"I don't know if that's necessarily the case, sir," Kevin said.

"No, no," Keller interrupted. "I pride myself in knowing when a person has grown, and you are on your way young man. Just outstanding. Really."

"Thanks … I guess," Kevin said. He shifted in his seat as a weird feeling crept into his gut.

The feeling wasn't wrong. Everything felt forced and disingenuous. Even Keller knew he couldn't keep up the act much longer.

"Listen, Kevin," Keller said. "I come to you with an odd request. I'm trusting that you will grant me this favor, and in return … perhaps I could be of assistance to you."

"I don't get it. Am I in trouble or something?" Kevin asked.

"No Kevin, my boy," Keller said. "Not in the slightest. You see … well … the matter at hand pertains to my wife, Eva."

Those familiar alarm bells began to ring again in Kevin's head. Now this was becoming awkward. Kevin had often seen people caught in love fueds but never had he participated in one.

"Sir. I don't think that I'm the right person to speak about this with," Kevin said. "Maybe talking to her would help. She seems like she really loves you."

Keller scoffed. "Love," he said. "It's so strange. Love. How it works. The other day she approached me and asked me if I believed in true love. I couldn't answer. You see, Kevin. Eva can be a bit sensitive in matters of the heart. Needless to say, she also has a very bad side."

"A bad side?" Kevin asked. "I don't think she's—"

Keller laughed. "So she has you fooled already?" he said. "My, she is good. And did she also tell you of the affair she had?"

The admission made the motion in the room stop. Kevin looked at Keller and knew he was serious. Even worse, he knew Keller was telling the truth.

"We don't talk about it much," Keller said. "Even though it was recent. She would never tell me who it was. My suspicion is that she was with someone at this very school."

"Sir, this is all too much, really," Kevin said.

"Now, Kevin. This is where I need you to come in," Keller said, his eyes bulging. "I need you to be in my corner. I have reason to believe that she is committing another affair, but I haven't been able to find out if I'm right. I need to know if it's true, and if so, with whom she is having the affair."

"You want me to … spy on her?" Kevin said. He adjusted his tie. "Sir, I couldn't possibly—"

"Eva told me of your session with her," Keller said. "She told me you were a good person. She also told me that she opened up to you. If anyone can do this, I know you can. She trusts you now."

Kevin paused. "I can't, sir," he said. "It's not right. I would be abusing that trust."

Keller's pause was equal in length to Kevin's. He leaned further across his desk to get a good view of Kevin's eyes. Every muscle in his face now reverted back to a stern and emotionless mask. The friendly atmosphere from earlier was sucked out of the room as Keller cleared his throat.

"Let me make myself clear, Mr. Deer," Keller said. "If you will not fulfill my request, I will be forced to expel you."

"You can't do that," Kevin said.

"Oh, but I can," Keller said. "And not just you, Kevin. Oh no. That would be too kind. Your friends will be expelled as well. You will find out with whom my wife is having an affair, or you'll face the consequences."

Kevin put his head down, defeated, and Keller celebrated by taking another peppermint to punctuate the bittersweet moment.

☙

Claire pushed back as Paul continued to kiss her. She refused to connect with him. It was clear things were different than when they had first started dating.

"You gonna tell me what's bothering you?" Paul asked. "You've been acting strange the last few days."

"Oh really?" Claire said. "Maybe it's because *you've* been acting strange for the last few weeks." Claire knew it wasn't right to shift blame back to Paul. She knew he was having a hard time dealing with everything that happened with his sister. But she couldn't help it. She wasn't ready to explain why she was acting strangely.

Paul looked at her as if he didn't recognize her, and then looked away. "That's it," he said. "I need to take a walk. Adios babe. Let me know when you're ready to stop acting like a child."

A mixture of sadness and frustration showed in Claire's eyes. She wished she could say this was the first time they had an argument, but it wasn't. This was their pattern for the last few weeks. He had become distant and withdrawn. To make matters worse, Eva's recent words kept flowing through her head. *They all are* repeated like a bad radio station. This was how she viewed Paul now. Just another guy. He turned and walked away without looking back at her. Claire reacted the only way she knew how: she stormed into her dorm room and slammed the door. She wanted to cry, but she was interrupted by a knock on her door. She rushed to it, hoping to receive an apology, but instead found herself awkwardly looking down at her visitor, who was nowhere near Paul's height. It was Sam.

"Why are you looking at me like I'm a criminal or something?" Sam said.

He made his way inside and dropped into the chair next to her computer desk. An open bag of chips sat there, and he grabbed it to help himself. Claire shut the door and rolled her eyes.

"Well, geez Sam," Claire said. "Come right in and help yourself."

"Thanks," Sam said as he munched on the salty chips.

Claire decided to ignore the inconsideration and lay on her bed to relax, but Sam's crunching kept her from doing so. She lifted her hands from her eyes to see him staring.

"Sam. Why?" Claire asked. "This really isn't the best time."

"Yeah…" Sam said. "Well … I need Kubo's book," he continued, ignoring Claire's obvious request to leave her alone. "It's kind of important."

"For what?" Claire asked, scowling at him.

"Nothing," Sam said. "I just need to do some research … for a class."

Claire didn't believe him for a second. She knew the look on his face all too well. Sam started getting nervous as she looked deeper at him.

"What are you hiding, Samuel Plimley?" Claire said, as she stood up and hovered over him.

"Why do I have to be hiding something?" Sam asked. He wiped the salt from the chips on his pants. "Maybe I'm just trying to get back on track with school. Or maybe I'm just trying to be responsible for once."

"I smell lies," Claire said, and she pinched Sam's nipples through his shirt.

Sam yelled. This was often the routine when Sam or Kevin gave Claire a hard time. They would play unassuming and their punishment would be twisted nipples. It was a mildly violent way of keeping the harmony.

"Okay, okay!" Sam said, rubbing his chest from the pain. "You win. God. I hate when you do that." Sam was only being half honest. Part of him enjoyed the attention.

Claire smiled and sat back on her bed, proud that she had accomplished her task. "So what do you need it for?" she asked.

"It *is* for school," Sam said.

Claire raised her eyebrow and rolled up her sleeves for another attack.

"Okay. Okay," Sam said, covering his nipples with his hands. "It's for Eva Keller."

"What do you mean 'It's for Eva Keller?'" Claire asked. "Sam, you didn't tell her about—"

"No. I swear I didn't," Sam said. "I never told her anything. She already knew about the book."

Disturbing feelings mixed in Claire's stomach. She did a double take at Sam to reassure herself that she wasn't the only one who felt strange about what Sam was bringing up. She was. Sam appeared clueless about Claire's haunting epiphany.

"Are you sure about this?" Claire asked.

"Yeah. She asked me about it," Sam said. "She's a really cool person once you open up to her."

Sam looked at Claire. The paleness on her face was that of fresh snow. Energy sparked in her pupils and she became enraged.

"I won't be opening up to that psycho anymore," Claire huffed, crossing her arms on her chest. "Don't you see it, Sam? *Eva is Z.*"

☞

Not a single drop of energy remained in Kevin after he left Keller's office. This quest was putting him through quite the ordeal, and now he was being extorted. He proceeded to the administration desk to schedule his next meeting with Eva.

"So … who died?" said the admin.

Kevin looked up to see a girl with a lavish appearance. Her focus was drilled into her phone as she typed with lightning speed; her fingers and wrists were covered in a plethora of gold bracelets and rings. Her hair and makeup looked just as expensive. In fact, everything on her did. Everything but her cheap plastic work badge—it read Iris Gordon.

"Who died?" Iris repeated as she looked up from her phone and smacked her gum.

"What makes you think somebody died?" Kevin said.

Iris looked at him up and down with a point of emphasis. It was her way of alluding to the obvious.

"Oh. I get it," Kevin said. "Umm. Yeah. No one. Just not my day I guess."

Iris shrugged her shoulders and handed Kevin a clipboard. He scribbled his name begrudgingly. Other than Iris's thumbs tapping on her phone, it was the only sound in the room. The silence was soon interrupted, however.

"Kevin?" Eva said. "Signing up for another session?"

Kevin looked up with an uncomfortable smile. He looked to his left and saw Dean Keller staring at him out of his office window. He realized he was trapped.

"Yep. That's me," Kevin said. "Signing up. Another session, yep."

Kevin looked at Iris, who looked at him as if he had just spoken in another language. Eva smiled and thought nothing of it.

"Good," Eva said. "I'll see you at our scheduled time, then."

Eva sauntered off, clearly in a good mood. Dean Keller walked away from his corner of the window. He must have been pleased that he'd gotten his way. Kevin was finally able to catch his breath.

"I get it," Iris said.

Kevin looked at her nervously. "You get what?" he asked.

"The whole therapy thing," Iris said. "I get it. You probably have some crazy weird things going on and you're being forced to take it. Am I right?"

"Sounds about right," Kevin said.

"Tell you what," Iris said. "You got twenty bucks?"

"Umm, I think so. Why?" Kevin asked.

"Well don't just stand there … give it here." Iris said. She extended her right hand and opened and closed it to signal to Kevin that he needed to put something green in the palm of her hand quickly.

Kevin dug through his pockets and pulled out whatever crumpled bills he could find. He didn't know why he was giving her money, but he hoped she would perform some sort of miracle with it. After he dropped it into her hand, Iris slowly and carefully unfolded it before stuffing it into her bra and then proceeded to press a series of buttons on her keyboard.

"There. You're all set," Iris said.

"Uh … sorry … I don't get it," Kevin said. He scratched the back of his head. "You pretty much just took twenty bucks from me. Is there some kind of magic that's supposed to happen or something?"

Iris popped and smacked her gum. She gave Kevin a confident nod as she turned her computer screen toward him and sat back, proudly crossing her arms. On the computer screen was a calendar tool that Kevin figured represented the holy grail of Eva's schedule. Kevin noticed that Iris had put him down for two sessions a week instead of three a week.

"I maneuvered Eva's schedule. Dean Keller checks her calendar, so he will think you're going to three sessions, but

I've hidden the third session from Eva, so to her, she thinks you only have two scheduled," Iris said. "Trust me. The dean will never know the difference. The two of them don't talk to each other, so they won't figure it out."

"Umm wow. Thanks. That's really cool of you," Kevin said. "But why would you do that for me?"

"What can I say?" Iris said. "I love a chance to make some extra cash. Besides, you're kind of cute. In a stressed out, pathetic sort of way."

Kevin didn't know how to take the strange compliment. He wasn't sure if he should feel good or, well … pathetic. But whatever moment of sparks that might have been, Iris soon ended it with another loud smack of her gum.

"Now get out of here before we both get in trouble," Iris said, and she gave him a wink and shooed him out of the room.

Kevin nodded in thanks and agreement. It was the first time anyone in that office had actually done something nice for him. And although he would have liked to believe that his day would end in a bit of luck from the friendly encounter, he was soon met with another misfortune. He looked at his phone as he exited the building and saw two new alerts flashing across his screen. He had two new text messages. One was from Claire. The second text was from Z.

> From Claire at 3:02 pm: Get here ASAP. We know who Z is.

> From 617-682-7897 at 4:36 pm: Oh ye of little faith. Don't you know I have you right where I want you? The cancer is spreading ;-) —Z

Flocks of unassuming students passed one another like vehicles on the cobblestone. The trees in the open corridor made for good shade. Some would say that it was a beautiful day. And for the most part, it was. However, there was an unsettling feud brewing on campus, and there was no mistaking it. On one of the campus courtyard benches, Sam sat across from Claire and Kevin with his arms folded tightly on his chest. It was a heated meeting. The three had never been so serious before. Perhaps it was because this time, for once, they felt like they had a good hunch who Z was.

"I'm not doing it," Sam said. "Eva's not Z. She's a good person. Why am I always in the middle of this with you guys?"

"You do not get the chance to be selfish right now," Claire said. "Sam, this is serious. For once we may have a good lead. Don't you find it a bit suspicious that we have been called to therapy sessions with her? And that when you get there, she asks about the book?"

"Why do we even need to figure out who Z is?" Sam asked. His voice was getting louder. "Why can't we just focus on getting Kevin through this?"

"That's the point," Claire said. "Z has been doing nothing but trying to sabotage this entire thing. Why can't you see that? If we can get you to trick Eva into revealing that she is Z, then maybe we have a shot at confronting her and making this stop."

"Nope. Not doing it," Sam said, folding his arms tighter.

"God. Why am I the only smart one? I can't deal," Claire said, throwing her hands in the air. "Will you please step in?" She stared at Kevin.

Kevin looked at Sam and found that he admired his friend's unwavering stubbornness. He had known Sam for years, they both had. But he had never seen him like this before. Kevin thought he could see a possible reason for Sam's tenacity.

"Sam," Kevin said. "Why won't you help? Tell us. What's the real reason?"

Sam looked at Kevin, then at Claire. He wished they understood how he felt. With his arms still crossed, he turned his eyes to the ground as embarrassment set in.

"You have feelings for her, don't you?" Kevin asked.

"Please not that," Claire said as she shook her head. "Anything but that."

Sam's silence said it all. Bright color filled his cheeks as he realized his secret was out.

"Sam. There's no way you can be with her," Kevin said. "For a few reasons but I'll just name the big ones. One, she's married to Dean Keller. Two, she's a campus counselor and that is *super* illegal. And three, she's like almost three times our age!"

"So it's fine for you to date and find love?" Sam said. "But when I finally find someone, suddenly it can't happen anymore? Why can't I be happy too?"

"But Sam, she's not what, or who, you think," Kevin said.

"You don't know that," Sam said, and he snapped his head up at Kevin. There was an energy in Sam's eyes.

Kevin could already sense that his friend was upset. Adding more fuel to the fire by revealing Keller's secret would only make it worse right now.

"This is ridiculous, Sam," Kevin said. "You're not going to date her. I won't allow it."

"You … you … you can't tell me what to do!" Sam shouted, and he lunged at Kevin.

Claire was shocked to see so much spirit and strength in him. He pushed Kevin to the ground and they rolled around like brothers often do. Neither of them was good at fighting, so it looked and sounded like two people just getting dead leaves on their clothes.

Claire rolled her eyes. "Men," she said.

She wanted to pay attention to the scuffle to determine who won once they got tired, but her attention was soon diverted. In the distance, she saw Eva sitting on a bench, looking at her phone, wearing her big black sunglasses to keep herself from being recognized. Claire noticed, though. She thought it was odd for Eva to be in the same area they were in, and immediately wondered if she knew that her true identity had been discovered.

"Guys," Claire whispered loudly so as not to attract attention to her voice. "Guys!" She snapped her fingers at them.

Kevin and Sam paused their fight to look up. Claire gave them both a look of frustration.

"Don't make it obvious, but I think Eva is watching us," Claire said. She shifted her eyes in the direction of where Eva was sitting.

Kevin and Sam both carefully looked around and saw what she was referring to. They sat still in shock. The coincidence of Eva being there seemed to confirm Claire and Kevin's suspicions, subjecting Sam to a harsh reality.

"I told you," Claire said. "That's it. I'm going to talk to her now."

"Claire," Kevin said.

Before he could stop her from going any further, another familiar face arrived to complicate the puzzle—it was Paul. He quickly approached Eva and embraced her as she stood up. The hug appeared more intimate and was much longer than appropriate; Kevin and Sam looked at Claire to guage hre reaction. Claire was speechless as she watched Paul and Eva venture off to the far end of campus. Claire saw them brushing their hands together as they walked away—and her cheeks burned and water began to fill her eyes.

"So it's true," Kevin said. "Keller was right."

"What?" Sam asked.

Kevin sighed. "Keller threatened to expel me unless I spied on Eva for him. He suspected her of having an affair. This may be what he was talking about."

"We need to follow them," Claire said. She wiped away the tears that were starting to fall down her cheeks.

☙

As the evening sun set, mischief hung in the crisp night air. Kevin, Claire, and Sam were sneaking around campus and now hiding in bushes near the observatory, waiting for the coast to be clear. It had been an hour now since Paul and Eva had gone into the observatory together, an hour during which few students or patrons visited. It was the perfect cover for any secrets. Their hearts were beating at the same rate—one moment with uncertainty, the next with courage. Regardless, they all felt that they were embarking on the final chapter of Z and her evil doings. It was a feeling that made the bushes feel comfortable as they waited.

Kevin looked at Claire and noticed her rocking back and forth as she crouched behind the bushes. Before he could let her know that everything would be okay, their suspects finally emerged. Kevin signaled Claire and Sam to keep quiet.

They were close enough to hear the conversation.

"When will I see you again?" Paul asked, hugging Eva.

"Ugh. We can't keep this up," Eva said and traced her pointer finger down Paul's chest. She pretended she wanted to get away from Paul, but she let him effortlessly pull her in closer to him. "We can't keep doing this. You know what I must have."

"And you know what I want. I want *you*. Screw everyone else," Paul said.

Claire balled her fists up so tightly that her knuckles turned white. Kevin noticed and put his hand on her shoulder. It wasn't the right time. They both knew that.

"You'll text me with what I asked for darling?" Eva said as she let go of Paul's embrace.

"Sure," Paul said.

Eva gave her usual mischievous smile and walked off, the sound of her heels fading into memory as she passed from view. Paul rested his back against the wall and watched her walk away, his eyes following the movement of her hips back and forth. He looked up at the night sky with a large grin plastered across his face, as if he had just won a sporting event. He looked around to see if the coast was clear and walked off in the opposite direction from the way Eva had gone. It was then that Claire chose to strike.

"I think I'm going to handle this one on my own," Claire said.

Kevin and Sam nodded in sympathy. There was no denying the obvious. Eva was having an affair with Paul. The unfortunate part of the matter was that it directly affected their friend.

"Hey, Claire," Sam said as he and Kevin watched her trot off. "Throw a punch in for me."

Claire smiled. She appreciated the support. And as she jogged away after Paul, a mountain of thoughts rushed through her head at once. Rather than let her emotions dictate the conversation, she chose to play it calm and stay collected—she hoped that she could remain level headed.

She quickly found Paul texting away near a remote part of the campus. Her plan to remain calm was out the window. As soon as she saw Paul, the hurt and confusion bubbled to the surface, and it led the conversation.

"She must be really special," Claire said.

Paul was caught off guard and almost dropped his phone.

"Claire. Uh … what are you doing here?" Paul said. "I was literally about to call you right now. I've missed you, babe." Paul clicked his phone to the lock screen and put it in his back pocket.

"Oh yeah?" Claire said. "Is that so? So you hanging out on campus at weird hours and flirting with my therapist—is that how you show me that you miss me?"

Paul sighed, the defeated sigh of somebody who had been caught. He knew there was no lying his way out of this.

"Claire, please," Paul said, as he took a step towards her with his arms open wide. "I can explain."

"How can you do that to me, huh?" Claire said, trying her best to not cry. She smacked his arms away and shouted at him. "I feel like such an idiot!"

"*You* feel like an idiot?" Paul said. "How do you think I feel? You think I'm crazy about coming in second place? I'm an athlete, Claire. We don't come in second place to anything. Or anybody."

"What are you talking about?" Claire said, even though she knew what Paul was getting at.

"Oh, come on," Paul said. "So you're going to play it off like you don't know what I'm talking about? Seriously? Okay, I'll admit it—I'm a jerk. That's kind of who I've always been. But at least I admit it. When are you going to admit it, Claire? I mean, Kevin comes around and you turn into a different person. You're alive when you're with him. Anyone can see that. Especially me."

Claire put her head down. Not because she was ashamed, but because he was right—every word of what he'd said was true. And no matter how much she tried to replace her feelings for Kevin with Paul, the surges of love's almighty power would continue to push her back to what was true in her heart. Even still, she would not admit it out loud. She couldn't.

"So what now?" Claire asked.

"You asked me yesterday why I was so distant," Paul said. "I'm leaving Cambridge, Claire. After everything with Libby, it's been too much. I can't stay here anymore. Well, unless …"

Claire looked back up at Paul. His eyes were focused on her.

Paul paused and took a nervous gulp of air. "Unless you can truthfully tell me that you don't love him," he said.

Claire put her head back down. Both of them knew it was over. Their short-lived relationship was now revealed to have been built on something that was never real. Paul scoffed. Claire felt every bit of his disappointment, hurt, and frustration.

"At least admit it to him," Paul said as he walked off. "You deserve that much."

Claire watched as Paul marched off into the evening. He faded away just as she would let her memories of him fade. She found the short moment to be sad, yet deep down she always knew it was inevitable.

Then she looked at her phone and saw a message that made her feel as if she had been punched in the gut.

> From 617-682-7897 at 9:11 pm: The Cancer is spreading. The Cancer is spreading :-) —Z

☽

The sun had sunk beneath the horizon. Most students were nestled into their beds or buried in their books as sprinklers and rustling leaves complemented the world around them. It was a solemn time. Kevin and Sam took a break from looking over the observatory deck to see that Claire was finally joining them. She looked as if she was in peaceful spirits. They knew what had happened with Paul without even having to ask. So they didn't. Claire accepted the silent invitation and joined them, leaning on the balcony.

"Can you believe this is where it all started?" Claire said. "Who would have thought that a simple book could turn into all of this."

"You tapping out?" Kevin asked.

"Are you kidding?" Claire said. "Attempted murders, suicides, psychopaths—I'm having the time of my life!"

Everyone laughed. It was true. Being at the observatory had awakened the pleasant memory of how it all had come about.

"I want to get this creep back," Claire said. "We have to get her back for all of this."

Kevin and Claire looked at Sam. A quiet shroud of reluctance hung around him. He was apprehensive. Still, in light of the new discovery and Eva's treachery, a sense of justice also burned within him. It was just enough to give him the vigor he needed to look his friends in the eyes. He nodded.

"I'm in," Sam said. "What's the plan?"

"Way to come through, Plimley," Claire said. She rubbed the top of his head and mashed his hair down. "Okay, she approached you about Kubo's book right? So we're already in the perfect situation. All you have to do is—"

"Wait," Kevin interrupted Claire. "Sam shouldn't be the one to do this. Keller would only expel him. It should be me. Besides, we can frame it part of my undercover act. He'll at least understand that."

"Well, that settles it," Sam said. "Now we just need the right gear. Claire, do you think you can score one of those mini cameras from somebody in the journalism club?"

"I think so," Claire said.

Claire looked at Kevin and smiled. She admired him stepping up to the plate, and Paul's words now came back to her. Her feelings for Kevin were more clear than ever. It was time. She needed to admit the truth.

"Kevin?" Claire asked.

Kevin couldn't hear her. A stranger in the distance had captured his attention. He felt something eerie in the air and turned to see that someone in a dark grey hoodie was watching from the dark corner inside the entrance to the deck. Claire and Sam noticed Kevin's face and looked where he was looking. It was a creepy sight, and one that only lasted for a quick moment, for as soon as they noticed the cloaked figure, so did the figure notice them. The figure pulled their hoodie further down their face and ran down the observatory stairs.

"Hey who's there?" Sam yelled as he started to run in the mystery person's direction.

It was too late. They rushed back to the deck to see if anyone had exited the observatory from downstairs, but they saw nothing. Nobody. Whoever it was is long gone by now.

"Maybe it was just a student being nosey?" Claire could feel the untruth in her suggestion but felt she had to offer up some sort of reassurance.

Kevin looked off into the distance. "Yeah. Maybe you're right …" he said.

"All right guys," Sam said. "Let's just forget it. Time to start mapping this out. I have an idea."

꙳

Eva raised one of her perfectly manicured eyebrows at Kevin. He could tell she could read through his demeanor, so he did his best to keep his suspicions from her.

"Oh my, Kevin," Eva said. "This is so sweet of you."

Kevin watched as Eva unwrapped a stuffed teddy bear. It was a simple yet meaningful gift. For Eva, the bear represented a late birthday present—one that, under the circumstances, she had a deep appreciation for. For Kevin, the bear represented his freedom. His nerves were tight as he hoped she wouldn't figure out the true meaning behind the gesture. If she did, she would have discovered a tiny camera nestled in the center of the bear's *Happy Birthday* sweater. And what a nifty little contraption it was. Just barely visible to the eye, disguised as a button. Kevin anxiously waited as Eva decided where to place the bear. He had anticipated that she would put the bear directly onto her desk so that it would face them head-on. She did just that, which allowed Kevin to relax back into his chair.

"You know," Eva said, rubbing the bear's furry ear, "you're actually the only person who got me something for my birthday."

"It's not much," Kevin said now feeling guilty. "It's just a bear."

Eva smiled. "Shall we begin?" she asked.

"Sure," Kevin said.

But nothing more could be said before Eva began to cry.

"I have a confession," Eva said. "I know more about you then what you may think. You see, Kevin, I was there … I was there the moment you had that horrible experience with Susan on Senior Recruitment day."

Kevin's eyes would have fallen out of their sockets if they

hadn't been connected. A few thoughts began to race through his mind. He wondered if this was the precursor to a confession. The question was, what was she about to confess? Would she admit her affair, or would she admit that she was the cyber-terrorist who had threatened him since day one of his journey? Either way, nothing could truly have prepared him for what she did reveal.

"I was there. And I felt every moment—every word you said. It inspired me, Kevin," Eva said as salty tears began to trickle down toward her lips. "You know, a lot of people say a lot of things about me in this school. And that's fine. They can have their moments. But truth is, I've been nothing but loyal and accommodating to a man who has never loved me. I've taken care of him and I've stayed by his side, even when I had finally found someone who did truly love me."

Eva wiped her tears away and shook her head in slight dismay. As she reflected on the one person who truly did love her, she became disheartened.

"After your speech," Eva said. "I made a personal vow. To find true love and finally be free. And I did. But my husband, well … he's not a quitting man, as I'm sure you very well may know. He's determined. So determined. He refused to let me leave. And I don't do well with confrontation. So, I eventually abandoned the one true man who loved me, and I will forever regret it. But when you came along, you … you inspired me again. I now feel like I need to do the right thing. For me. Despite my husband. I need to do this for love. For James. "

Kevin couldn't believe it. "James … as in James Kubo?" he asked as he tried to process all of these moving pieces.

"Yes, that James," Eva said. "He loved me. He would go on and on about this book he wrote that he believed would help us be together once and for all. But I didn't believe it. Not until Paul—your fellow junior classmate—told me about it in one of our counseling sessions. He told me everything that he heard you guys doing. It was then that I knew there was really something to the book. I tried to get more information out of Paul, but he wanted more from me than what I was willing to give—he asked me to skew his grades so that he could pass junior and senior year with straight A's. I just couldn't agree to that. It wouldn't be fair.

"Even if the book possessed nothing of the sort, it was the last memory I would have of my dear James. "

Kevin was stunned. It was like someone had ended a concert in the most triumphant fashion. And as with that concert ending, there was also a bitter sorrow that followed—the realization that it had ended in the way you least expected. Kevin now knew without a doubt that Eva wasn't Z. This new revelation left him puzzled and guilty for assuming the worst in her. As their session ended, he realized that he had voided everything out but her passionate confession. She lightly placed her hand on his arm as he walked out of her office.

"Thank you, Kevin," Eva said and she gave Kevin's arm a squeeze. "It's guys like you that give a woman like me hope again."

The collar on Kevin's shirt felt tighter than usual. He went to adjust it in hopes that doing so would somehow ease his guilt. It didn't. He looked back at the bear he had deceived her with and imagined how crushed she would be if she discovered the camera inside it. He needed to do something, and quick.

"So I'll see you at the same time next week?" Eva asked.

"Yep. That works," Kevin said.

It was too late. Eva smiled as she closed her door. All Kevin could do was sink further into his guilt as he checked out at the admin desk. Iris, as usual, was typing away at her phone—the only difference was that she was wearing a brand-new sparkling Rolex watch.

"Someone die again?" Iris asked.

"Not yet," Kevin said. He looked towards Keller's office. "Hey. I don't suppose twenty bucks would score me the key to get into the offices late tonight would it?"

"Not a chance," Iris said. "But forty will."

Kevin nodded as he handed the money over. Iris dug through the messy drawer of her desk, pushing aside crumpled papers and old mint tin. After a few seconds, she presented Kevin with two rusty keys—one for Dean Keller's office and the other for Eva's. Plan 'B' was now in effect.

☽

"This is just nuts," Sam said as he kept watch. "I hope you're right about this. I'm tired of sneaking into places."

"Would you just keep an eye out?" Kevin muttered.

With a bit of effort and elbow grease, the old spare key eventually did its job. Kevin, Claire, and Sam were officially in the main offices for the dean and student services. They were lucky. It appeared not a single soul was there.

"Are you absolutely sure about Eva?" Claire asked. "You're sure she's not Z?"

"I'm positive," Kevin said. "You guys are going to have to trust me on this."

Everyone agreed.

"So what's the signal if any of us spot trouble?" Sam said.

"I don't know," Kevin said. "Maybe just make like a bird call or something."

"A bird call? In the middle of the night?" Sam asked. "Yeah, that's believable."

"Shut up, Sam. Geez," Claire said. "Just make any sound. We'll figure it out one way or the other."

"Okay, so … you guys ready?" Kevin asked.

"Yep," said Claire and Sam in unison.

It was like bad clockwork, but clockwork nonetheless. Each of them went on to take charge of their assigned role for "Plan B." Claire, who still thought that Eva could be behind Z, took the other spare key from Kevin to turn over Dean Keller's office. Kevin's objective was to retrieve the camera-equipped teddy bear from Eva's office. And Sam … well, Sam had the most important task of all. He would use his uncanny senses to keep watch at the door and make bird calls if he had to in order to alert the others about newcomers. As he waited outside the main door, he practiced a few whispers, like the pigeon noises he often heard on campus.

The problem was, despite all the careful planning that had been done in the last three hours, they were wrong about several things—the most important of which would soon be discovered by Kevin.

As he opened the door to Eva's office, he was comforted by the quiet. It made him feel safe enough to flip the light on. He closed the door and nearly fell over backward as he discovered Eva hiding behind the door. She put her fingers to her lips and signaled him to be quiet.

"Kevin?" she asked in a low voice. "What are you doing here right now? You shouldn't be here. How did you even get in?"

"Sorry. It's kind of a long story," Kevin said. He was concerned. "But what are *you* doing here? Why were you here in the dark?"

Eva sighed. "I'm hiding."

"Hiding?" Kevin asked. "From who?"

"Keller," Eva said. "I did it Kevin. I left him. I'm going to pursue true love for once. It's all because of you. Your advice."

"Wait, what? No!" Kevin said. "I never meant for you to leave him."

Before Eva could answer, the two heard a collection of annoying bird calls just outside the door. Kevin knew that wasn't a good sign. He looked at Eva and tried using his eyes to communicate the potential danger.

"You should hide," Kevin said.

She wasted no time and locked herself away in the closet furthest from the window. Kevin, however, had now become completely distracted in the unfolding drama and had forgotten to hide. He scrambled to find a place, but there wasn't enough time. The office door opened with enough force to blow stacks of files and papers across the room.

"Where is she!" Keller yelled. His eyes were bloodthirsty and spit flecked his lips.

"I don't know what you mean," Kevin said, as he backed up against the closet where Eva was hiding.

"Don't you play dumb with me! I saw the text messages," Keller said. He towered over Kevin and looked him square in his eyes. "You. It was you all along wasn't it?" You convinced her to leave me. You filled her head up with all of this bogus 'love' nonsense. You were the one who plotted to meet her here, and *YOU* were the one who had an affair with my wife!"

"No, sir, please … let me explain. That is not what happened," Kevin said. His back was fully pressed against the closet, and he had his hands out in front of him.

"Consider yourself expelled," Keller's voice boomed in the small counseling office.

Kevin paused—he was in shock. He looked at the door and saw Sam and Claire standing in the door frame.

"But not until after I break your legs," Keller said. He grabbed Kevin by the throat and yanked him toward the center of the room. Kevin's friends pulled on Keller's clothes to get him off, but as much as he appreciated their courageous efforts, he found himself losing his grip on consciousness.

"Stop!" Eva screamed. She pushed the closet doors open and stumbled over toward Kevin and her soon-to-be ex-husband.

Keller stopped what he was doing immediately. Eva looked at him with hurt in her eyes.

"Alex! What are you doing?" Eva shrieked—she was afraid of him. "This is madness and it stops now!"

"I got the text messages," Keller said. "They told me to come here. That I'd find you with *him*." He gritted his teeth together and pointed at Kevin.

Sam butted in. "Umm, these texts messages wouldn't have happened to come from some weirdo named Z … did they?"

"So it was you!" Keller said.

"No. No. No," Sam said. "That's not us."

"Look, Alex," Eva said. "We can't do this. Who are we fooling? Look at who we've become. It's time to let this go."

The rage began to burn in Keller's eyes once more. Everyone seemed to notice except Kevin, who was still dazed from suffocation.

"You're not leaving me," Keller said. He grabbed Kevin again by his stiff white shirt collar and cocked back his fist for a punch. "If I can't have you … no one will."

Kevin's haze made the slow moment seem that much slower. Keller's fist flew through the air like a bomb falling from a plane. There was no question that the blow would render him unconscious. With what energy he had left, he closed his eyes. It was all he could do to keep from imagining the final impact. He waited. More time went by, and so he waited some more. There was nothing. He noticed the tight grip on his collar had loosened, so he opened his eyes to figure out what had happened.

To his amazement, Keller was slumped in Eva's office chair, out cold. There was blood rushing down his forehead, and he moaned in pain as he clutched his head. Kevin looked at Claire and Sam, who were fixated on Eva. Kevin turned to her. She huffed and puffed as she tightly gripped a heavy owl-shaped brass paperweight. The blood on it indicated that this had been the weapon she'd struck Keller with.

"You guys need to leave," Eva said as she dropped the paperweight. "Now!"

"What about you?" Sam asked.

"Don't worry about me. I'll sort this out," Eva said. "For now you guys need to leave."

Everyone understood why and they appreciated what she was doing.

"Eva you really don't have to—" Kevin said.

"Go. I'll be fine," Eva said. "I've been dealing with this brute for the last seven years."

Kevin looked down at Keller, who rolled over in pain. He looked back at Eva and smiled. He shared a quick glance with Claire and Sam, and they were off. Their only hope now was that this would be the last of the madness.

☙

Neither Kevin, Claire, or Sam said much the following evening. All of the drama from the counseling sessions and their after-hours fight with Eva and Dean Keller had rendered them lifeless—they felt like zombies as they tried to process everything that had happened. The stars overhead were the only thing that provided any comfort. Sam was the only one who had an appetite, but even to him, the pizza tasted bland. They all felt guilty. Both Eva and Dean Keller lost their jobs over the commotion, and the three friends couldn't help but feel like it was all their fault.

"All that for what?" Kevin said. "We didn't catch Z, we got an innocent lady fired, and now the journey is failed. With all of this happening, I didn't have time to find my Cancer." Kevin tossed his half-eaten pizza slice back onto the paper plate in front of him and wiped the grease on his pants.

Everyone shared Kevin's frustration. They too had invested just as much. It wasn't like them to give up on things, especially when there was a pact that bound the initiative. They were so close, yet so far. Everyone took a deep breath at the same time. It wasn't until Claire noticed a blinking light from Kevin's phone that things began to glimmer with hope.

"Well as if things couldn't get any worse, there's always the bad news you're probably getting on your phone right now," Claire said.

"What do you mean?" Kevin asked. He picked up his phone and hoped Claire's pessimism wouldn't be confirmed.

"No way," he said, staring at his screen.

Kevin had received an e-mail directly from Eva. Claire leaned in close to Kevin to read what he was reading; Sam was preoccupied with his own phone.

E-MAIL FROM: EVA.KELLER@THERAPYWORKS.COM

My Darling Kevin,

Words can't describe how you've changed my life. It's funny because even in writing this, I think of how humorous and odd it may seem to you. But you've truly touched me, Kevin Deer. From the moment you got on that stage and made me a believer in love again.

You made me believe in myself again. Now that I am free, I feel like I owe you these words. You were a good friend and listener. I will never forget you.

Love Always,

Eva

Kevin looked up from his phone at Claire. "Does this count as my Cancer?" Kevin asked.

Claire laughed and shook her head—she was astonished. "I guess it does," she said. "I can't believe this. This is insane. Like seriously."

"Oh, Claire," Kevin said as he gave her a hug. "We did it. And I have you to thank. You've always been there for me."

Claire melted. All she could do was take it all in. And yet, even with a hug like this that made her forget about everything around her, she felt alone. They looked at each other and Claire turned away. She couldn't keep torturing herself like this.

"Kevin—" Claire said.

"What the!" Sam yelled, interrupting Claire's second attempt at sharing her true feelings with Kevin. "Guys! You need to check this out."

Sam squeezed his way in between Kevin and Claire.

"Okay, so remember how we put the camera in Eva's teddy bear?" Sam asked.

"Yeah, why?" Kevin asked.

"Well, I synced the camera to this app so we could get access to the whole video feed just in case the bear got lost or something. I've been playing back the footage of the whole fight scene with you and Keller. Look," Sam said.

Sam handed his phone to Kevin. Claire leaned in.

"So what's the big deal?" Claire said. "We've seen this already."

"No," Sam said. "I mean zoom in. After the bear falls down. It points toward the window."

Kevin used his fingers to zoom in on the screen. Each time he pinched his fingers out, the image got bigger and bigger, and a haunting realization came through to each of them.

When the bear fell over, it was able to get a clear view of the window facing the courtyard behind Eva's office. A person wearing a dark grey hoodie, similar to the one on the mystery guest they had seen before in the observatory, glared through the window. Nothing could be made out, just the hoodie and their intense aura. The image gave all of them goosebumps.

"I bet you that's Z," Sam said forcefully.

"I bet you're right," Claire said. Even though the mystery person's eyes could not be seen, Claire felt like she was being watched intensely, and she cringed as if to hide from them.

Kevin chuckled. Both Claire and Sam looked on, confused. Kevin, who was pressing the boundaries of insane behavior, stood up and walked to the edge of the observatory balcony. He thought of everything that had led up to this point: Susan, Professor Kubo, Laura the Aries, Professor Thompson, Gracie the Taurus, Libby the Gemini, Paul, Dean Keller, Eva the Cancer—all the glorious madness that had transpired to give him the confidence in who he was at that exact, defining moment.

Kevin's chuckling turned into full-blown laughter. Claire and Sam sat in silence, unsure what was happening. Kevin turned to them and shouted, "I'm going to find love!"

He continued in between his laughter. "I'm going to find it. If it's the last thing I do. But for now, I think we've had enough signs that have shown me it's time to focus on my Senior Year."

"But Kevin …" Claire started to make the case for continuing the quest, but quickly realized she was putting her foot in her mouth, and so she just mumbled, "Nevermind."

"Guys," Kevin said. "It's not that I'm afraid of what is to come. I am. But as I sit here and reflect on the last few months,

I realize that the incredible adventure and the encounters with everybody I had come to love were born out of that fear. But I think, for now, we might need a break. Let's take our final exams and then enjoy our summer vacation. I'm ready to find love when it's ready to find me."

Kevin stared at the stars in the sky and draped one arm around each friend. "Let's embrace our new year, with or without love. What do you say?"

Claire and Sam looked at each other and then at Kevin. "Deal," they said.

As the summer night came to a close, the three friends were ready to say goodbye to their junior year and start their last year at Cambridge High School Boarding Academy. They had much to look forward to this senior year—homecoming, winter formal, prom, and college applications and acceptance letters.

They pushed aside their Zodiac plan and pledged to make Senior Year their focus. Claire looked at Kevin with new respect. Sam looked at Claire with new emotions. The three of them may not have fully understood the reasons behind the series of events that had taken place, but one thing was certain—they were in it together, no matter what.

The hidden stranger who spied on them from the shadows nearby went unnoticed. Kevin, Sam, and Claire began the walk back to their dorms, ready to leave everything behind and move on.

THE END

...OR IS IT?

Kevin laid down on his small dormitory bed after a long night of studying for his last exam before summer break. Just as he closed his eyes, a light from his cell phone flickered. He instinctively wanted to ignore it, but chose to look at it after the fourth alert. A small sense of fear set in as he read the messages.

> From 617-682-7897 at 2:11am: So you think this is over?

> From 617-682-7897 at 2:11am: You think that's how it works?

> From 617-682-7897 at 2:11am: You think you can just walk away and everything will go back to normal? Such wishful thinking!

> From 617-682-7897 at 2:12am: If only it were that easy. :-)

> Sent at 2:13am: I don't want any problems. I just want to be left alone.

> From 617-682-7897 at 2:12am: My my. I expected more from you Mr. Deer. Your journey has only just begun.

> Sent at 2:13am: Listen. I'm done with the quest. You got what you wanted.

> From 617-682-7897 at 2:13am: When the next eight mistresses arrive, which they inevitably will, be sure to be careful. I'll be watching. This isn't over until I say it is. Nighty night. ;-)

Kevin didn't dare send another reply. He put his phone face down next to him and looked at the ceiling. All he could do was think to himself. *What am I going to do...*